Someone Talked

R. CONRAD STEIN

Historical background, page 141
THE WORLD WAR II HOMEFRONT

CHIRON BOOKS

Someone Talked
A ChironBooks historical novel for young readers

Cover and interior design © 2011 by Pat Perrin.

"Someone Talked" poster. See page 139 for information about
the poster used on the front cover.

This is a work of fiction. Names, characters, places, and incidents
either are the product of the author's imagination or are fictitious
representations of historical figures and events.

Publisher's Cataloging-in-Publication data

Stein, R. Conrad.
    Someone talked / R. Conrad Stein.
    p. cm.
    "The World War II Homefront"
    Summary : During World War II, young Dan and Tony are
suspicious of foreign accents and strange behaviors, but
tracking a "spy" leads to a shocking discovery.
    ISBN 978-1-935178-17-0

1. World War, 1939-1945 --United States --Juvenile fiction. 2.
United States --History --1933-1945 --Juvenile fiction. 3. Chicago
(Ill.) --Juvenile fiction. 4. Refugees --Juvenile Fiction. I. Title.

PZ7.S8216 So 2011
[Fic]   Library of Congress Control Number: 2011939826

Manufactured in the United States of America
ChironBooks, Chapel Hill, NC   **www.chironbooks.com**

*I dedicate this book
to my wife, Deborah Kent Stein,
and to my daughter, Janna Mary Stein.*

Chapter One

"Ya see that sign?"

Tony Avellini pointed to a victory poster hanging on the wall at Meyer's Drugstore. The poster showed a freighter, its bow pointed high out of the water, sinking fast. Near the ship swam a drowning sailor desperately trying to keep his head above the waves. Bold letters over the poster said: SOMEONE TALKED!

"Sure," said Dan Zelinski. "I've seen it a lot of times."

But he didn't mention that each time he saw it he shivered. That freighter could be his father's ship. The drowning sailor could be … He did not want to complete the thought.

"The sign means you ain't supposed to talk about ships because a German spy might hear you," Tony said. "Them spies, they're all over the place." He looked left and right as if expecting to see an enemy secret agent hidden in a corner of the drugstore listening to his every word. "If you don't watch out them spies will tell the submarines, and the subs will sink our ships."

Dan kept his eyes away from the victory poster because its message filled him with fear. Still he tried to talk sense to his friend, and that was never an easy task.

"Look, Tony, here in Chicago the sign doesn't mean ships. The German subs can't get here." Then Dan spoke in a voice just above a whisper. "There's that factory across the street, the one where my ma works. You know what they make there?"

"Yeah. They make bomb ... bomb things."

"Shhhh," Dan cautioned, putting his finger to his lips. "They make bomb sights there, but we're not supposed to know that." He too looked around to make sure no one overheard his words. "The government, they didn't have a sign that said 'Watch Out for Spies Who Want to Blow Up Factories.' So they put this ship sign up here."

Tony thought about that answer and nodded his head in agreement. "Right. It's because them factory workers come over here and have ice cream after work. And a German who wanted to blow up the factory could hang around here and pick up tips."

They both nodded, knowingly, as if they had just shared a deep and vitally important secret.

It was early August in 1944, and the United States had been at war for two-and-a-half years. To Dan and Tony, both twelve years old, it seemed as if World War II had been raging all their lives. Only dimly did they remember "normal times," the days before the Japanese attack on Pearl Harbor. For Dan, normal times meant his father was home and working as a janitor for the Lafayette Apartment Hotel on Milwaukee Avenue. Now his father was on a ship on the Atlantic Ocean where, again he shivered, German submarines lurked.

"Let's go to Lincoln Avenue." Tony said after they left the drugstore.

"Why?"

"There's lots of stuff there we can look at. Come on, let's take a walk."

Dan hesitated when Tony said the word "stuff." Often that word, when used by Tony, spelled trouble.

"Ya know, sometimes I hope the war never ends," said Tony.

"What do you mean?" Dan snapped. "People are getting killed. I haven't seen my father in two years. That's all because of the war."

"Don't get me wrong. I don't like to see guys getting killed and all," said Tony. "But I figure after the war, they're gonna have a lot more cops. They can't get cops now because all the men are in the Army. And besides, our mothers are going to be home more and asking you where you been all the time. Now they're too busy to ask you a lot of questions."

Tony's mother also worked in a factory on the night shift. His father … well, they didn't talk about him much anymore.

"Cubs are playing the Cardinals today," said Dan, trying to change the subject. "I think they're going to win the pennant this year."

"Fighting the Germans, that must be tough," said Tony. "They got big cannons and tanks and all."

Dan looked at Tony and saw that familiar, dreamlike stare he'd seen so often before. Tony was no longer peacefully walking along a sidewalk in Chicago. Instead, Tony crept over a battlefield somewhere in Europe, stalking the enemy. In his mind he carried a rifle and had a couple of hand grenades hanging from his belt. That's the way his imagination worked. Tony's inner thoughts took him to a different world where he lived fantastic adventures and did heroic deeds.

Dan tried to steer the conversation back to baseball.

"My father, he loves the Cubs. He loves them so much he says crazy things about them. I remember once, he was listening on the radio, and the Cubs lost a close game and he said, 'Them Cubs, they ain't going to win another World Series, not for a hundred years.' But that was just talk. I mean, that's impossible. No team can go a hundred years without winning the Series."

Tony remained an ocean away, locked in furious combat with the German army. Dan could almost hear the explosions: Boom! Crash! Kablow!

"Look," said Tony pointing at the Diversey Avenue bridge that spanned the West Branch of the Chicago River. "If a German blow-up guy, you know, what do they call them?"

"Saboteur?"

"Yeah, sab, saba ... blew up that bridge, you couldn't drive trucks across it. Then the Germans would win the war."

Actually, that didn't make sense. The Diversey bridge was just one of maybe a hundred bridges that crossed the Chicago River. The Germans would have to blow up all of them to even come close to winning the war. Still, Dan let Tony's mind spin like a merry-go-round. That way, any time he wished, Dan could hop on and take a ride.

"I know where the Germans live--Lincoln Avenue," said Tony. Then he drew a deep breath.

"He … he used to take me to Lincoln Avenue a lot."

"He" meant Tony's Uncle George. Neither Dan nor Tony mentioned the name much because it was the only thing that made Tony cry. Before the war Uncle George owned a horse and wagon. He named the horse Mussolini to scorn the dictator of Italy who he said was a horse's rear end. When Dan and Tony were little they'd sit on the back of the wagon and ride the alleys looking for junk which Uncle George picked up and sold to scrap dealers. Uncle George claimed he could tell the kind of neighborhood they were in just by the smells. "There's Greeks living here," he'd say. "Smell that olive oil." Then the war started. Uncle George went into the Army where they put him to work driving a truck. Everyone in Tony's family was relieved, figuring he had a safe job. He got killed in North Africa when his truck rolled over a land mine.

They walked another half hour, exchanging few words. Tony walked all over the city. Sometimes he'd walk from the Logan Square neighborhood, where they both lived, all the way downtown. That was a two-hour trip through a maze of streets. Still, he always got there and never got lost.

"Here we are," Tony announced. "Lincoln Avenue."

Dan thought of Chicago as a small version of Europe. Streets were borderlines. Cross a street and you go from Poland (his neighborhood) to Germany (the Lincoln Avenue neighborhood). Still, nothing looked different here. The sidewalks on Lincoln Avenue were lined with stores that had apartments above them, just like Milwaukee Avenue in his neighborhood. Dan took a sniff of the air, like Uncle George used to do. His nose detected nothing German.

Dan, too, had a rich imagination, but he kept his dreams locked up inside him. Silently he wrote movies about the war and other history-making events. He never wrote anything on paper. Still, his made-up movies were so great, so exciting, they won the Academy Award. Tony, on the other hand, was a doer who created a world with his dreams and then lived in that world. Why was it that God made some guys to be dreamers and others to be doers and so few to be complete people? In his thoughts Dan always asked God a blizzard of questions. Sometimes, when he couldn't find answers, he got mad. He even got mad at God.

"Let's look around," said Tony

It was just after four o'clock. The sidewalks were empty because people were working in their factories. Every Chicago neighborhood had factories where drill machines whirled and punch presses pounded. You could hear the clatter of machinery even when standing outside on the sidewalk. Factories made rifle parts, uniforms, bullets, bombs, and the thousand little springs and screws that went into airplane engines. The tons of material that flowed out was part of an enormous drive called the war effort, the holy mission to smash the Germans and the Japs.

Someday Dan would write a movie about the factories and the men and women who worked in them. He'd show the workers smiling as they churned out the tools of war. In the movie's final scene a tough-looking factory guy puts the last part on a machine gun, then stands back to look at the gun and says, "Take that, Hitler." Wow-- one of Dan's movies just won another Academy Award.

"Let's see what's in here," Tony said, pointing to a store.

It was a butcher shop, nothing more. Sawdust covered the floor to absorb blood that soaked out of the meat. Because of the August heat the shop's doors were open. Twisting bands of fly- paper hung from the ceiling. Dan watched a fly circling around the paper. He felt like shouting out a warning: Don't land! Get away from that sticky stuff! But the fly touched on the gluey paper, struggled for a second, and died. What a sad way to go, even for a fly. The paper was pep- pered with scores of dead flies. It was a regular fly graveyard.

"Look at all them sausages all hanging from the wall on them strings," said Tony pointing. "Boy, the Germans love their sausages."

"So do Italians and Poles."

"Yeah, I know, but these Germans really like them."

This was a typical discourse with Tony. Ger- mans really like sausages. End of discussion.

The place had five or six customers, all of them women who were too old to hold factory jobs. Two butchers worked behind the counter cutting chunks of meat. Everyone spoke a foreign language, which Dan presumed was German. In one hand the customers held money. The other hand clutched books of wartime ration stamps that limited how much meat a family could buy in a week. For many people the ration stamps were more precious than cash.

Tony said in a hush, "You see, if we could get a couple of them sausages, the ones that look like hot dogs, we could take them outside and build a fire and ..."

"Hey, don't take anything," Dan whispered back. "You'll get us in big trouble."

"It's just stuff, something small from a store like this. It's nothing."

"No. No. Not this time. The last time we almost got killed."

"Don't worry. It's from the Germans, and we're at war with them."

"I'm leaving right now."

Dan hurried toward the door. Not again, he told himself. Not again.

"Hey you! Punk! Stop where you are." One of the butchers, a big beefy man with a red face, shouted at them. "Ach du lieber!" said the other butcher, an older guy, who was even fatter.

Tony had grabbed five or six hot dogs that hung curled around a hook. He no doubt thought he could break them off and race outside without being seen. But the casings that held them together were as tough as a rope. He pulled. The hook fell off the wall and hit the floor with a shocking crash.

Dan saw the customers, a hundred pairs of furious eyes, all locked on him, staring as if he were the mastermind of this grand theft. He read what the eyes said: That little savage! Lock him up! Put him in a cage!

"Run for it!" yelled Tony.

Chapter Two

Nobody seemed to mind when Dan and Tony built a fire of sticks and milk cartons in an empty lot off Lincoln Avenue. This was wartime. No adult had a spare moment to stop and correct the behavior of a couple of troublemaking kids. Men and women hurried along the sidewalk probably thinking those two boys had to be crazy to stand around a fire on an August afternoon.

Dan poked a hot dog onto a stick and held it over the fire.

"Lookit. Look at that hot dog," said Dan in a scolding voice like an annoyed school teacher. "See how the skin makes blisters and the whole hot dog turns black. That's what hell is like. You're in a fire and you just burn up like that. You scream and scream, but you still burn up. That's where you're going, Tony, straight to hell."

"What do you mean? Why am I going to hell?"

"Because you steal. That's a mortal sin. You know that."

"Hey, I don't really steal. I just take stuff now and then, you know, from a store, a place that's got lots of stuff anyway. I mean, I never take nothing from another person."

"It's still stealing."

"No it ain't. It's just, you know, taking stuff."

Stuff. Dan should have run home when Tony first said the word back in their own neighborhood. He could picture Tony on Judgment Day standing before God Almighty and claiming there is a difference between "taking stuff" and "stealing." God would shake his head sadly and then push Tony into a bright orange lake of fire.

Sister Theresa, who taught Catechism, used to warn the kids about hell and all its agonies. She was a tiny woman from the Philippines who spoke in a clipped accent: "Theenk of the pain you feel when you acceedently burn your finger on a stove. Then imageen that burning pain all over your body. Imageen, too, that the pain will last forever and ever, an eternity of hell's fires, theenk of it."

Tony roasted two hot dogs on his stick. He was smiling as if he were opening a gift on Christmas morning. He should know all about the terrors of hell because he was in Sister Theresa's class, sitting at the next desk. But Tony lived in his own world.

At least this time they had no harrowing experiences. The men in the butcher shop were too old and too fat to chase them. Last summer Tony took--took, of course--ice cream bars from the back of a Good Humor truck driven by a wiry-looking Greek guy. The guy chased Dan and Tony down Milwaukee Avenue threatening to cut their throats when he got his hands on them. They escaped only by dodging through a complex of walkways between the buildings of their neighborhood. Good thing Tony was an escape artist, like a magician in the movies.

"Mine's done," said Tony.

He pulled his hot dogs out of the fire, touched one with the tip of a finger, and snapped his hand back from the heat. Then he took a bite while it was still on the stick.

"Mmmmm, good."

Dan let his own hot dog cool before he ventured a taste. Yes, it was good and juicy, but the taste was the wages of sin. How can you enjoy food that was stolen? This hot dog was his damnation, his ticket to an eternity of searing flames.

"Mmmmm, good," said Tony again.

"Mmmmm," said another voice.

Who's that? Was it the devil? Dan turned. A boy who was about his age stood on Tony's left. He was thin and slight, almost to the point of being sickly looking. He wore grimy pants and a smudged T-shirt.

Even Tony was surprised. "Who you?" He turned to Dan, "Who's this guy?"

Dan shrugged his shoulders. But in his darkest fears this kid was an usher, like a movie usher, who would lead him into the terrible world of hell. Yet he did not look like the devil. The boy stood without saying a word. The expression on his face reminded Dan of a dog cocking its nose while trying to puzzle something out.

"Want a hot dog?" Tony said.

The boy said nothing.

"Tony, I don't think this guy can talk," said Dan. "Maybe he can't talk English.

"You talk English?" Tony shouted the words as if he reasoned talking loudly would get through to the boy.

Nothing.

"Maybe he's German," said Dan, "and he only speaks the German language. You said this is a German neighborhood."

Dan thought it was bad manners to be talking about the boy as if he were a car and they were trying to figure out the make and model. Tony had no such worries.

"Naaa, he don't look German to me. Look at his hair, black like mine. Germans are more

blond. Maybe he's a Dago like me. You talk
Dago? Capeech?" Tony did not speak a word of
Italian, but in his imagination he was fluent in
the language.

Again the boy said nothing. He did not look
at the hot dogs, indicating to Dan he wasn't hungry. Maybe he's hungry for something else. Hungry for a friend?

"I got these hot dogs at the butcher shop
where all the Germans go," Tony said. Then he
added with a sly smile. "I bought them there."

Looking down at his toes, the kid said, in
almost a whisper, "German."

"Naaaa, you don't look German to me," said
Tony.

Dan figured this boy--whatever his national-
ity--must be at least a bit crazy because of the
way he just stood there saying hardly a word. It
was astonishing the way Tony always attracted
nuts. Wherever they went, loony people came up
to Tony. And Tony talked to them, too.

"Me and my friend, we're not from this
neighborhood," said Tony. "We live over in Logan
Square. We're looking over the Germans around
here."

That's the way Tony always talked. When he was caught up in his dream world he didn't care what outlandish stuff he said, and even to perfect strangers.

"Thomas! Thomas, you go. You go from fire."

An old man with greying hair stood in the alley. He wore a black overcoat even though it was a muggy day. The man leaned on a cane, then picked the cane up and shook it over his head.

"You hear me, Thomas. You come. Here come right now." His accent was thick. He pronounced Thomas TohMASS.

The silent kid, Thomas, took a few steps backwards. Slowly, almost fearfully, he walked out of the empty lot to join the man wearing the overcoat. The old guy's face was red with anger. "Come. Come." he said. "I tell you many times. You no talk. You talk no one."

"Wow," said Dan. "Old Overcoat there, he's sure mad at Thomas."

"Let's follow Overcoat and the kid," said Tony. "We'll do it like the detectives in the movies. They won't even know we're following them."

"Yeah, let's go."

Shadowing these two characters detective-style was an adventure Dan would have never thought of on his own. But Tony's fresh ideas rolled along like a freight train. At least this was something that couldn't get them into real big trouble. Dan felt giddy with thrills as they hid behind fences and peered over garbage cans, all the time keeping a watchful eye on the two. Overcoat and Thomas seemed to have no idea they were being followed. Anyway, Overcoat wouldn't have noticed since he was screaming at Thomas in a language Dan did not understand.

On Lincoln Avenue, Overcoat stopped and fumbled in his pocket for keys. He opened a door next to a tavern and shouted at Thomas to get in. The door banged shut behind them. Tony and Dan tiptoed up to the door and pressed their faces against the tiny window. All they saw was a set of stairs that led to an apartment above the saloon. Bolted to the brick wall next to the door was a mailbox and a doorbell button.

"Look at this," Tony said pointing at the mailbox. "There's no name on it. Everyone's got names on their mailboxes. Everyone except ..."

Dan knew what Tony was thinking. "A Spy. You mean Overcoat is a German spy."

"You got it."

"Wait a minute, Tony, just because old Overcoat doesn't have his name on his mailbox, that doesn't mean much."

"That guy, Overcoat, he ain't from Chicago. Where do you figure he's from?"

"Maybe Germany," said Dan. "I guess he was talking German."

"See!"

"But there's lots of Germans around here."

"Yeah, I know that too," said Tony. "But then there's that Thomas. There's something about him that makes me think he knows a lot." Tony started clenching and unclenching his fists as if he were grabbing for words. "I think he knows stuff about spies and all, but he's too afraid to tell us."

Where does Tony get these ideas, thought Dan. The guy has to really believe in those ideas in order to get so caught up in them. He envied his friend's ability to live so completely in that special realm created by his fantasies.

"I want to come back here right away tomorrow." said Tony. Then he stepped back to read

the name on the tavern window. "The Hof...
Hof..." He couldn't pronounce it.

"The Hofbrau House," said Dan. "I'll bet that's
a German word."

Dan knew almost nothing about languages.
He was Polish on his father's side and Irish on
his mother's, so he grew up speaking only English at home. Maybe one of these days, after the
war, he'd travel around the world and learn six
different languages. People respect you when
you can talk a bunch of languages because that
proves you're smart.

Just then Tony got a glint in his eye.

"Hey, remember when we were little kids on
Halloween, when we'd ring all the bells in an
apartment building and then run out the door
while they were all buzzing us in?"

Dan nodded. That's what they did when they
were very little, before they graduated to other
Halloween stunts like tipping over garbage cans
and tying buckets to car bumpers. Dan noticed
Tony eying the doorbell button on Overcoat's
apartment.

"No, not with this crazy guy. Old Overcoat might shoot us with a gun."

Tony pushed the button and leaned on it for a half minute. In return, the buzzer sounded.

"Run for it!" shouted Tony.

Chapter Three

It was after six o'clock when Dan returned to his block, Wisner Street off Milwaukee Avenue. Wisner was a pleasant tree- lined side street. He and his mother lived on the second floor of a two-flat. The bottom floor was occupied by the land-lady, Mrs. Swanson. Her first name was Helga, but out of respect Dan and his mother always called her Mrs. Swanson. She was a nice woman who lived alone, all because of the war.

Dan walked up the porch steps and looked at Mrs Swanson's front window. The blue star was still there. She hadn't had the heart to change it. Flags bearing blue stars stood in the windows of many houses and apartment build-ings on Wisner. A blue star meant you had a

family member--a son, a daughter, or a father-
-in the armed forces. The O'Brien family down
the block had a flag with four blue stars on it,
representing their four sons, all of whom were
in the Navy.

One or two houses on Wisner had gold stars
in the windows. That meant someone from that
household had been killed in the war. Teachers
and Catholic nuns told kids they should stop and
say a silent prayer whenever they saw a gold star
hanging in a window. Mrs. Swanson could put
up a gold star because her son, Ernest, a Marine
lieutenant, died on that awful little Pacific
island called Tarawa. That happened a year ago
and Mrs. Swanson still had not taken down the
blue star and put a gold one in its place. Dan's
mother said she never would do that. A gold star
would remind her of things she wanted to chase
out of her thoughts: her boy was dead, her husband died shortly after the son, and now she
was alone, All this because of the war.

Dan let himself in with his key. When the
door was halfway open, he stopped suddenly.
Something smelled scrumptious, something
baking in the oven.

"Mom?" Dan called.

"Yes, I'm home for a change."

"Wow, I didn't think you'd be home." He pointed to the kitchen. "What's cooking?"

"A cake, strawberry, your favorite."

"Wow."

Then his mother hugged him.

"I'm tired of working nine, ten hours every day. I don't have any time for myself, and I don't have any time to spend with you."

"What about the war effort?" said Dan, with a smile.

"Let someone else win the war, at least for tonight."

She did not ask Dan where he had been, what he did, or who he ran around with. Those were questions for normal times. These days kids were expected to stay out of trouble without being hounded by their parents. Dan was glad she asked no questions. He knew she did not like him hanging out with Tony Avellini at all, not one bit.

"Besides, I got to clean up this place tonight," she said. "This apartment is beginning to look like an unholy mess. But what can I do? I work for the Slave Brothers all day long and then come home too exhausted to really clean this place."

Slave Brothers was the nickname for the factory where she worked. Actually it was called Sloff Brothers, Incorporated. The employees said it was the Slave Brothers because, they claimed, the people there had to work like slaves.

Dan and his mother ate together, a wonderful supper of pork chops, mashed potatoes and gravy, and corn on the cob. His mother complained the pork chops cost twelve ration stamps. She didn't even mention the price in dollars and cents. The cake for dessert tasted like it was baked in heaven. If only Dan's father were eating with them it would be just like normal times.

His mother must have guessed what Dan was thinking. "I wonder what your father is doing now?" she asked.

Dan wanted to say something pleasant, but no words came out. After a two-year absence his father was more a framed photograph hanging in the front room than he was a real man. Still,

Dan remembered his laugh that sounded like a lion's roar. When Dan was small they used to play the Laughing Game. Dan would do something funny, like fall on his bottom, while his father sat with a frozen face trying to keep from laughing. Always his father lost the Laughing Game. Now Dan pictured the man on a rolling deck in the middle of the Atlantic. What about the submarines? What about the spies who told the Germans of ship movements in the Atlantic? SOMEONE TALKED!

In his mind, Dan wrote a new movie. He'd call the movie SOMEONE TALKED!, and it would be a lesson for citizens to be always on the alert for spies. The movie will start with a loud- mouth dock worker sitting at a drugstore soda fountain eating ice cream. This foolish guy is talking about a ship he loaded this morning with guns and tanks. Behind him lurks a shadowy man scribbling notes on a little pad of paper. The man wears a black overcoat even though it is a hot day. Overcoat is smiling, an evil smile.

Then the scene shifts. The audience sees a sailor, Dan's father, alone on the deck of a ship.

The sea is rough. Mighty waves wash over the ship and a howling wind sweeps the deck. Far in the distance the man, his father, spots a submarine periscope poking above the water. He shouts to the captain, but his voice is drowned out by the roar of waves and wind. Then, suddenly, the man sees the white trail of a torpedo arrowing directly at his ship. What is the man, his father, going to do now? He can only stand, helpless, as the torpedo slams into the side of his ship and explodes with a terrible blast. But how can Dan figure a way to get his father's ship out of this fix so the movie can continue? Dan's movie stories always ran into stumbling blocks like this.

"I miss your dad. I miss him so badly." Dan's mother said. "Here I am, another war wife waiting for her man to come home. This darn war."

She never swore. "Heck" and "darn" were the most reckless words she ever used. And she said those words only when expressing her feelings about World War II.

"But they attacked us," said Dan. "The Japs bombed us and then the Germans wanted to fight. Now we got to win the war."

"Right, that's what I've heard for … for what seems to be forever." She twisted the wedding ring on her finger. "Sometimes, I don't know. Maybe we should have given them Pearl Harbor if they wanted it so badly. We could have sold it to them or something."

"Ma, we couldn't do that."

"I never even heard of Pearl Harbor before. None of us had ever heard of the place. I remember your father and I sitting right here in this living room and looking at a map, trying to find it. Then all of a sudden this crazy place, this Pearl Harbor, is the most important place in all of our lives. It just seems unfair."

She turned to look out the window and down toward the first floor apartment. "I think about Ernest a lot lately, too. He was about as nice a young man as you'll ever meet. I mean, he was a big, handsome boy, always smiling, always happy, and now … I think of him and I wonder if all this is worth it."

Ernest, Mrs. Swanson's son, used to play football for Lane Tech high school. He was so good he won a scholarship to the University of

Illinois. Sometimes at night, under the street lights, he threw passes to Dan and the other kids. Usually high school football stars didn't want to play with small-fry kids, but Ernest was different. He liked kids. Ernest joined the Marines just two days after the attack on Pearl Harbor. So many thousands of men signed up in the wake of Pearl Harbor that the services couldn't process them fast enough. In time, though, the Marines accepted Ernest. And then they sent him to Tarawa.

Pearl Harbor, December 7, 1941, was the day that turned everyone's life upside down. Dan's father wanted to join the Army right away, but he was forty and the Army wanted only younger men. Now, in 1944, they were taking guys forty and older. Despite his age, his father insisted on doing his part to win the war. So he became a merchant marine, a crewman working on a ship. It was an even more dangerous job than being a soldier on the fighting fronts. Early in the war, ships were being sunk by German subs right off the east coast of the United States. People in coastal states like Virginia or New Jersey could see the stricken ships out there burn-ing at night. But now Dan knew the American Navy was strong, and our ships were blasting the German subs out of the water. Still, being a merchant sailor was a job filled with hazards. German submarines continued to sail under the Atlantic and spies operated everywhere. SOME-ONE TALKED! SOMEONE TALKED!

Dan's mother turned and smiled. She had such a pretty smile. "Want to listen to the radio? The Bob Hope show's coming on."

"Sure."

The show started with a song sung by a cho-rus saying Pepsodent toothpaste would perform miracles on your teeth. Then Bob Hope and Jerry Colona, his sidekick, began their string of jokes. They did a routine where Jerry was a Japanese army officer who was twenty-eight years old, and said he was going to kill himself on his next birthday. "Why are you going to kill your-self on your birthday?" asked Bob. "Because no Jap want to be twenty-nine." The radio audience exploded into laughter. Dan laughed so hard he had to bend over.

"I don't get it," said Dan's mother.

"You don't get that?" said Dan, surprised.

"No."

"The Jap is going to kill himself at age twenty-eight because no Jap wants to be twenty-nine. See." He picked up a pencil and wrote on a piece of paper, B-29. "It's a new airplane, a real big bomber, and it's going to start bombing the heck out of Japan."

"Oh, an airplane, I see."

Dan thought, wow, and she works at a factory where--rumors claim--they make bomb sights.

Suddenly there was a shout from the street. "Hey, get those lights out!"

"Who's that?" asked Dan's mother.

"Hey, don't you know there's a blackout going on?"

Dan and his mother looked out the open window. Standing on the sidewalk was old Mr. Schneider from across the street, who served as Wisner Street's official Air Raid Warden. His wife held his arm and appeared to be trying to tug him away. The old man was wearing his white Air Raid Warden's helmet.

"Put those lights out. You want the Germans to win this thing? You want Hitler to win this war?"

Mr. Schneider was born in Germany and came to the United States when he was a boy. Neighbors claimed that Schneider was the most ferocious Air Raid Warden on the North Side because he wanted to prove his loyalty was to the United States, not Germany. During air raid drills, his voice sounded like a foghorn as he roared at people to turn out their lights.

"I didn't hear anything about a blackout," said Dan's mother. "We haven't had a blackout for a year now."

Mrs. Schneider, a chubby lady dressed in a housecoat, said, "Look, please ignore him, he's been ..." Then, standing behind her husband, she made a motion like she was drinking a shot of whiskey. "He's not been well lately."

"Don't you know air raid drills are important?" said old man Schneider. "Hitler's going to win this thing if we don't watch out."

On the floor below, Mrs. Swanson the landlady opened her window. "What's going on out here? What's the matter?"

"Oh, Helga, now he's disturbed you, too," said Mrs. Schneider. "And you've got so much on your mind as it is. I'm trying to get this old fool home. He hasn't seen our boy in more than two years. I keep telling him the boy's safe. He's over in England with the Air Force, but he's just fixing the planes. He doesn't fly in them."

The old man now stood with his head hung so low his helmet was about to fall off. In a softer voice he mumbled about air raids, and the awful Nazis, and about how cruel Hitler was, and how we've got to be careful or he'll win this thing.

Dan thought back to the air raid drills and the night blackouts they had earlier in the war. Of course, the Germans and the Japanese didn't have planes that could come anywhere near Chicago. But the whole country, even Iowa farm towns, had the drills. Dan wanted more than anything to be a bicycle messenger and pedal written messages from warden to warden during the blackouts. Boy Scouts were chosen to be messengers. In Dan's troop, Alfie Diaz, who lived down the block, won the job. Alfie was a real drip. He impressed adults because he was always smiling and always polite. Goody-goody Alfie, Dan called him. On the street Mrs. Schneider led her husband home. "I'm so sorry, so, so sorry. Oh, how I wish this war was over."

It'll end, thought Dan. The war will be over soon if we all pitch in and work for victory. How he wished he were old enough to serve on the fighting fronts. The Schneider son is in England fixing the big bombers that take off with a sound of thunder and fly in heroic formations over Germany to rain bombs on Nazi cities. Dan had seen those mighty fleets of bombers on the war news at the movies. He wanted desperately to be there, but not fixing planes. He wanted to fly them, race over Germany, drop bombs, kill Nazis, end the war, and come home a hero. Maybe then somebody would make a movie about him, THE DAN ZELINSKI STORY: BLOOD AND GUTS

Chapter Four

Dan woke up the next day to an empty house. His mother was off at the Slave Brothers' making, he guessed, bomb sights. Today was Friday. He knew that because his weekly allowance, two quarters, lay on the kitchen table. He really didn't have to do many chores to earn that allowance because his mother was an old softy. All she wanted him to do was to stay out of trouble. That, of course, meant associating with Tony Avellini was a dangerous activity.

For a minute Dan rolled the two quarters on the table. If he truly wanted to help the war effort he'd use the money to buy War Stamps. Each ten-cent War Stamp helped to pay for the

bullets and bombs needed for final victory. But
Dan suspected he'd spend the money on movies.
The neighborhood theater, the Logan, changed
movies three times a week, and during summer
vacations he saw at least two of them. Half fare
at the movies cost twelve cents. Of course he
had to get popcorn, ten cents a box, and maybe
a candy bar at five cents.

No doubt Hitler was pleased every time he
wasted money at the theater instead of buying
stamps. Some day Dan would draw a victory
poster that would hang in Meyer's drugstore.
The picture would show a giant figure of Adolf
Hitler wearing a black overcoat. The Nazi dictator smiles as he watches a bunch of kids lined
up in front of the ticket window at the movie
show. Old Hitler says, "That's right, boys and
girls, don't buy War Stamps, fritter away your
money at the movies instead."

Dan turned on the radio and spun the dial.
He heard the familiar deep voice of Paul ... Paul
Somebody, an announcer who relished in the tell-
ing of war victories. The announcer said, "Yes-
terday the Marines landed on another Jap island.
They didn't disclose the name of the island, but

you can bet it's one step closer to Japan. Yeah, we got those Japs reeling now, by gum," said the man, sounding like he was at ringside describing a boxing match. "Yep, another landing or two and we'll knock them crumbs down. I mean we'll put them down on their Japan-knees." The radio announcer chuckled to himself over his "Japan-knees" joke.

Before the war Dan figured that the word "Jap" was a bad word. But now all the radio people used it. He once watched the news while at the movies and even Eleanor Roosevelt, the president's wife, said the word. A victory poster that hung in his school said: EVERY WAR STAMP YOU BUY KILLS A JAP.

On the radio Paul Somebody made an important announcement: Today, at the lakefront, the Navy was going to demonstrate its latest aircraft. The air show would start at noon, and spectators could get a good view of it off the Belmont Harbor. The planes were from the Glenview Naval Air Station where Navy pilots trained.

"But don't you want to go back to Lincoln Avenue today? That's where the German spies live." said Tony.

Dan met Tony in front of the Logan Theater on Milwaukee Avenue. They always met there. Not that they planned these meetings. The get-togethers just sort of happened every weekday during summer vacation.

"Lookit, this air show is going to be real keen. I'll bet they'll have a hundred planes there, maybe more.

"What's more important, the airplanes or catching spies? What about the war ... the war ... what's that word?"

"The war effort."

"Yeah, the war effort. That means catching spies, don't it? That guy, Overcoat, he's a spy. And that kid, Thomas, he knows all about spy stuff."

Tony had a point, even though Dan was too realistic to believe they'd ever really catch spies. Still, a true American citizen on the home front would be diligent about spy-catching duties and forsake the air show. Dan took a different approach in the conversation.

"Look, someday I'll help the war effort by being a plane- spotter, you know, one of those guys who looks into the sky with binoculars to spot bombers coming over the city. So I got to be able to tell our planes from the enemy planes, right?"

Tony said nothing, but clearly seeing the air show was not how he wanted to spend this day.

"Besides, look here." Dan pulled one of his quarters from his pocket. "I got some money, so we can take the streetcar to the lake."

Tony shrugged his shoulders. "Okay. I guess we can look in on those spies later. I mean, we know where they live and all."

Dan smiled. Now and then he got his way with Tony, but those little triumphs were rare.

Often Dan thought about the saying "opposites attract" when he pondered his friendship with Tony. They had met in kindergarten, but then Tony flunked a couple of grades so they were no longer in the same class. In every way imaginable they were opposites, even in their looks. Dan was skinny with frail, sticklike arms. He had brown hair and milky white skin. By contrast, Tony was stocky with broad shoulders and the arms of a wrestler. Tony's hair was shiny black. His face was shadowy to the point where it almost looked like he needed a shave. Dan often marveled at how the two of them could be so different yet remain such close buddies.

At the corner of Kedzie and Belmont they climbed on board the back entrance of a streetcar heading east. Dan held his quarter out toward the conductor.

"Two please," Dan said. "Two … two halves."

The conductor, a heavy, red-faced man, looked down on them. "So, it's two halves you tell me. And am I supposed to believe that fellow there," he pointed at Tony, "is under eleven years old? Am I supposed to believe that now?"

Eleven was the cut-off age between half fares and full fares on the streetcars. Both Dan and Tony were twelve. Half fare was seven cents and Dan didn't even know what full fare cost. He could always get on for half without question, but Tony looked so old he could probably buy a bottle of beer at a tavern if he wanted to try.

Not knowing what else to say, Dan thrust his quarter out again. "Two … two halves, please."

The big man sighed, took the quarter, and gave Dan eleven cents change. "Get along with you now, but don't think for a minute you fooled me."

Dan and Tony took a seat toward the front of the streetcar. To himself Dan said an Act of Contrition, the special prayer good Catholics recite when asking forgiveness for sins. Lying to a streetcar conductor, he figured, was a venial sin, one that would send him to purgatory. At least in purgatory, unlike hell, he could look forward to some end to his sufferings. Anyway, it was Tony who always insisted they pay half fare. Tony never worried about sin, hell's fires, purgatory, or any of those other fears that regularly tormented Dan.

As they passed Lincoln Avenue Tony said, "Hey, right down there. That's where the spy lives. What's the name of that tavern? The Hof … the Hof …"

"The Hofbrau House," said Dan.

"Yeah, that's it. The Hof. We got to remember that. We're going to catch them spies and maybe get a reward from the cops. Them spies are gonna make us a lot of money."

Sure, Dan thought. And Superman will join the Army and he'll overnight lead us to victory over the Japs and the Germans.

The streetcar rolled under the Belmont L station, where a troop of Boy Scouts formed two lines on the sidewalk. Dan figured they were heading for the lake to watch the air show. All the boys were colored. Their leader was a stocky old black man with a stubby white beard. No doubt they had just come from the South Side. That's the way it was in Chicago: the whites lived on the North Side and the colored on the South Side. As far as Dan knew, that's the way it always had been.

"Look at that, right from the South Side," said Tony. "Look at all them nigger guys."

"Don't say that word," Dan snapped. His voice was harsh, but he spoke in a whisper so no one else on the streetcar could hear him.

"What word?"

"The one you just said. My mother would slap me if I said that word around her." Then he looked around the streetcar, hoping he'd see no offended black faces. "You're supposed to say colored … colored people."

"Hey, I ain't got nothing against the niggers."

"Tony!"

"Wait a minute. I know the niggers." Then Tony cocked his head. "You know, from the time I was in The School."

The School was a code word they often used. A year ago Tony was sent to a reformatory for three months. He was sentenced there for "taking stuff" from a store. He didn't like to talk about his time there, and when he did he referred to the place as The School.

"My best friend at ... The School was a nigger kid, Leroy. Once a crazy Dago named Andy cornered me. This guy Andy and his boys, they ... they wanted to do something bad to me. But then Leroy and his friends come along and they chased Andy away. So I got nothing against niggers. I like them."

"You're not supposed to use that word," Dan insisted, again in a voice just above a whisper.

"But that's what Leroy and his friends called each other."

"Really?"

Dan was astounded to hear this. Did colored people really use that word to each other?

"Still, you're not supposed to say … you know what. It's colored. Colored people or Negroes."

"Was Leroy wrong?"

Arguing with Tony was exasperating. Dan decided to sit in silence for a while, hoping Tony would drop the subject. After five minutes the streetcar stopped at Marine Drive, and they got off. Ahead sprawled Lincoln Park and the lakefront.

To Dan Lake Michigan had to be like the Atlantic Ocean, where his father was now. The lake had waves and a constant breeze, and it cast a refreshing smell that filled the air for blocks away. Dan had never seen an ocean. In fact he had never in all his life travelled more than fifty miles from Chicago. One of these days he'd travel around the world, learn a half dozen languages, and meet people from everywhere. One of these days.

"Where's the airplanes?" asked Tony.

"The guy on the radio said they'd come over at noon. Just a few minutes now."

The planes were right on time. From over the lake came a buzz. Then some spots appeared in the sky. Like great black dragonflies the planes came, flying low and fast in tight formations. There must have been five hundred of them. People watching from the park gasped ooohs and aaaahs.

"Look at them," shouted Dan. "There's a bunch of Hellcats. That's the best fighter the Navy's got. And look at them over there," Dan pointed. "They're what ya call Avengers. They carry torpedoes, and the torpedoes sink all them Jap ships."

"Sure is a lot of airplanes," said Tony, sounding unimpressed. "Yeah, a whole lot of planes."

"And look there!" Dan was so excited he was now jumping up and down. "Those are Corsairs. See how you can tell? They got wings that bend low like a seagull or something. Wow, Corsairs are my favorite planes in all the world."

"Sure is a lot of planes," said Tony.

"Boy, I wish I was up in one of those Corsairs." Dan made a sound, dat-dat-dat-dat-dat-dat, like a machine gun. "If I was up there in a Corsair I'd shoot down all the Japs and I'd win this war. What do you think of that, Tony."

"Sure is a lot of planes."

"Airplanes."

Wait! Dan was so busy looking up at the fighters that he failed to notice they had been joined by Thomas, that strange kid they'd met the previous day.

"Airplanes."

Thomas wore the same dirty pair of pants and probably the same T-shirt. He stared at them, and this time he grinned. Dan noticed he was missing about a half dozen teeth.

"Airplanes," he repeated.

"Hey, what are you doing here?" asked Tony.

"Airplanes," he said again, pointing up to the sky.

The planes retreated, thundering over the Chicago skyline. All was quiet now except for waves lapping on the Belmont Harbor.

"What are you doing here?" Tony demanded from Thomas. "Did you follow us after we got off the streetcar? Are you a spy or something?"

"Lay off him," said Dan. "His neighborhood is right over there on Lincoln Avenue, not far from here. I bet he came over to watch the air show, just like us."

"Airplanes," said Thomas.

"See, I told you, he just came to look at the air show."

Suddenly a groundshaking roar shattered the silence of the lakefront. A squadron of six Avenger torpedo planes roared in from the lake and buzzed over Lincoln Park at treetop level. The thundering flight marked the official climax of the air show, ending it with what sounded like a bomb blast.

When the Avengers disappeared above the rooftops to the west, Dan looked about him. Where was Thomas?

"Thomas," Tony called out. "Where'd you go? Tom! Tom!" Then Tony put his hands on his hips. "Thomas, what are you doing down there? Get out."

To Dan it looked like Tony was talking to a bush. Wasn't there a Bible story about Moses seeing God in a bush? Finally Dan saw Thomas hiding under the bush, curled around its branches, and lying so still he looked almost like a lump in the Lincoln Park soil.

"Get out, Thomas. Come on, get out from under there." Tony reached down, grabbed the limp Thomas by the arm, and dragged him out.

"Don't treat him so rough," said Dan.

"I ain't being rough. I just want to get him out from that stupid bush. He can catch cold or something on that ground."

Thomas rolled on his back, and Dan saw his face was ghostly white.

"What's wrong with him?" asked Tony, clearly worried.

"It must have been the Avengers. Those planes came in so low and so loud they scared him."

"Hey, Tom, don't worry about the planes." Tony said. He suddenly sounded like a loving father comforting a child after the child woke from a nightmare. "Don't be scared. I'm here with you. We're here with you. The planes can't hurt you now."

"Airplanes," said Thomas. Slowly the color returned to his face. Once more he grinned through broken teeth. Thomas puckered his lips together and then made an explosion sound. He threw his arms out wide to indicate a bomb blast.

"Yeah, the planes drop bombs," said Tony. "The bombs explode, and they kill the Germans and the Japs. That way we win the war, see?"

Tony smiled and Thomas got to his feet.

"What about that guy you live with," said Tony, fixated on one subject. "That guy with the overcoat and the cane? That guy, he your father?"

Very slowly, Thomas shook his head no.

"Where is he now? You know who I mean. Overcoat."

Thomas pointed out of the park and toward his neighborhood on Lincoln Avenue.

"Is he home now?"

Again a slow headshake, meaning no, he's not home.

Dan wanted to run away from the park and get out of this conversation. This was all part of Tony's made-up games, the games that always went too far. Thomas lived with a spy. Tony intended to capture that spy and be a hero. There was no room for the real truth here. Tony was locked into his dream world and he shut out other thoughts.

"What does that man, old Overcoat, do all day?"

For a long moment Thomas was silent. Then he blurted out, "Radio."

"Radio? Does he listen to the radio?"

Thomas put his hand out and moved it gently up and down as if he were tapping on something. "Radio. Radio."

A dark and scary thought flashed through Dan's mind. "Hey, I don't think he means Overcoat is listening to the radio. Look at his hand. He means old Overcoat is clicking on a telegraph thing, you know, a telegraph key. He talks in code over the telegraph."

"Is that right? Does Overcoat talk on a telegraph thing?"

"Radio," said Thomas, again pretending to tap out code with his hand.

Wow, thought Dan. This really is something. Old Overcoat talks on a telegraph key that's wired to a radio. Who else but a spy would do that?

"Hey, Thomas," Tony said. "Let's go over to where you live on Lincoln Avenue and you can show us the radio."

"Today, no," said Thomas. It was the first time he uttered two words in a row.

"Okay, not today." Tony knew enough not to push his luck because this boy frightened easily.

"Look, we'll be over there on Lincoln Avenue in maybe a couple of days," said Tony. "You can tell us all about Overcoat and maybe show us" he whispered, "... you know, the radio stuff."

"You know where I live?"

Well, thought Dan, Thomas can even say a full sentence.

"Yeah, we sort of know," said Tony not wanting to admit that he and Dan had already spied on Thomas and Overcoat.

Without another word, Thomas turned and walked out of the park.

"See what I told you?" said Tony as they hurried down Belmont Avenue.

"Thomas is strange, but that doesn't mean he's a spy, or that Overcoat is a spy either."

Yet even Dan's skeptical mind was spinning fast now. What was all this about radios and telegraph keys and codes?

"Hey, that guy Thomas, he's trying to tell us things, but he can't ... he can't ..."

"Express them, tell the things right out."

"Yeah, that's right. I know why. I mean if I lived with a spy, I'd be afraid to talk about him, too."

A special radio you can send codes with. That's puzzling. No one Dan knew had such equipment in their houses. But there had to be some logical explanation. Surely there could be no German spy ring operating on Lincoln Avenue on the North Side of Chicago. That kind of stuff only happened in the movies. And even if old Overcoat were a spy, could a couple of kids like he and Tony catch him? Could we? Could we?

Chapter Five

It was Sunday morning and Dan hadn't seen Tony for two days. This was their usual summer vacation pattern. During the week they were inseparable. But on Saturdays and Sundays they did not see each other at all because Dan's mother was around the house to watch his comings and goings. He kept his friendship with Tony a secret from her.

Dan thought about sin more on a Sunday than any other day of the week. His mother disapproved of him hanging around with Tony, yet he did it despite her wishes. This was certainly a sin. But wait. What if it were his God-given duty to pal around with Tony and keep him from getting into big trouble? Friendships might be something created by God. Maybe you don't really choose your friends at all. Maybe God puts certain people in your path for you to meet and become pals with. That way your friends are sort of your destiny. To sin or not to sin. This stuff takes a lot of thought.

"All right, I'm finally ready, let's go."

Dan's mother looked pretty in her Sunday dress. It was a sunny day and as they walked to church Dan felt so happy he wanted to break out singing. Too bad they couldn't walk to church with his father the way they used to in normal times. His father had only one suit, and he always looked uncomfortable in it because he was the type who did not wear fancy clothes well. Yet every Sunday he put on that suit and paraded with his family down Milwaukee Avenue on the way to St. Hyacinth. It was as if he wanted to say, "Look everybody, look at my wife and kid. Ain't they great?"

This Sunday Dan and his mother met the Diaz family from down the block. It was customary to walk to church with neighbors. Dan walked with Alfie Diaz, Goody-goody Alfie, who buttered up the scout master into giving him the job of bicycle messenger during the blackouts. Since this was Sunday Dan felt a need to ignore past grudges. Besides, Alfie looked grim.

"We got something bad in the mail yesterday," said Alfie.

"What was it?"

"A letter from the draft board. They're calling my father in to take another physical exam for the Army. Last time he failed it because he got something wrong with his back. But now they're taking men with bad backs, bad feet, bad eyesight, everything."

Dan searched for something to say that would be comforting. It was his duty as a Catholic to make Goody-goody Alfie feel good, even though he thought the guy was a jerk.

"Don't worry, Alfie, maybe they won't send your father overseas. Look, he's a cab driver right?"

"Right."

"Then maybe the Army will have your father driving a jeep or a truck or something, you know, away from all the fighting." But Dan remembered that Tony's Uncle George was a truck driver and he still got killed, blown to little bits in North Africa.

Alfie hung his head low and spoke in a tone so soft Dan could hardly hear him. "No, I got a bad feeling about all this. I think he might go off to some base and then they'll send him overseas and we'll never see him again. That happened to a girl who lives around the corner from me. A real nice girl, too. The Army took her brother, and sent him overseas, and then … and then, nothing. She never saw him again."

This whole conversation was out of character for Goody-goody Alfie. Usually Alfie spoke of the great things he did in school or with the scouts. Now he was scared sick and ready to cry. Silently Dan forgave him for taking the bicycle messenger job that he so coveted. Never again would he call him Goody-goody Alfie.

In church Dan knelt, stood, and sat along with his fellow worshippers. He never knew when to do these things. Instead, he watched the person next to him out of the corner of his eye and did whatever that person did. Though he tried to be a good Catholic, the rituals of the mass baffled him. In his wild thoughts Dan figured he'd change all this stuff about kneeling and standing if he ever became the Pope. Sister Theresa, the tiny terror of Catechism class, said any good Catholic boy could grow up to become the Pope and head the Catholic Church. But all the popes Dan had ever heard of were Italian. Could a Polish boy ever become Pope? No, that would never happen.

Through the Mass Dan prayed for his mother. He worried that the war and her separation from his father was demoralizing her, causing her to lose her faith in God and the church. Fervently he asked God to make her understand this war was His will. World War II, Dan believed, was a holy crusade to destroy the evil Germans and Japs. That's what he'd heard since the war started. And it had to be true. Who could doubt God was on America's side?

"Come on. Let's listen to the radio," said Dan's mother later that night. "See what's on."

Dan looked at the newspaper. "Let's see. Sunday. Eight o'clock. Oh, look. The Lux Radio

Theater has a drama. It says here it's a story about a man who discovers the nice couple who just moved into the house next door are secret German spies. Hey, that sounds real good."

"Oh, I'm tired of war stuff. Isn't there anything else?"

"But we got to watch out for spies. They're all over the place," said Dan. He added in his thoughts--and they all wear black overcoats, too.

"There's got to be something else on the radio on a Sunday night like this."

Dan looked again. "There's," he took a deep breath, "'Your Hit Parade!'" he said the words triumphantly, like a radio announcer would. "All the top songs on--'Yooour Hit Parade!'"

"You're good," said his mother. "Maybe you should go on the radio one of these days."

"Maybe I will one of these days," said Dan. Silently he planned his future career in radio. But what was there to plan? Most radio shows were broadcast from a studio with no live audience watching. All you had to do is talk with a lot of enthusiasm, as if you're jumping for joy with every word. You could probably announce the stuff with your pants off and no one would know. What an easy job that must be.

They listened, sitting in the darkened room staring at the glowing radio dial as if they could see pictures there. One song followed another top-rated song on the always-popular "Your Hit Parade!" Many of the songs told stories of wartime loneliness: "I'll be seeing you." "I'll walk alone." The program ended with the announcer giving the usual radio farewell: "Bye-bye and buy bonds."

"Guess what?" said Dan's mother as she clicked off the radio. "When I went shopping a little while ago, I got something from a guy in a little store that I didn't have to pay stamps for. It's ice cream."

"Ice cream, and you didn't have to pay stamps? Ma, did you buy on the black market?"

His mother put her finger to her lips, "Shhhhh."

She went into the kitchen and took a carton from the icebox. They had to eat it now because there was no ice in the icebox and the ice cream would melt in a few hours.

His mother came out with two heaping bowls of fudge ripple, Dan's favorite. Already it was soft and beginning to melt. Dan pictured some guy making this black market stuff in his kitchen and then selling it to people who didn't want to spend the ration stamps a legitimate store had to charge. That dirty guy! How are we going to win the war if people buy and sell black market stuff? Maybe he should do his part in the war effort and refuse to eat the ice cream. He ate, wolfing it down. The contraband fudge ripple tasted delicious.

It was late. Dan was ready to go to bed. His mother was in her pajamas and robe. Suddenly a loud knock sounded at the door.

"Maria, it's me, Helga. Come downstairs right away. Your husband is on the phone."

An eerie silence gripped the apartment. Dan heard his mother taking deep breaths.

"Is he okay?"

"Yes, he sounds fine."

"Where's he calling from?"

"I don't know. Come on, quick."

Dan's family never had a telephone. Before the war his father said they couldn't afford one.

Now, when they had money, they couldn't get a phone because all the telephone equipment was being used in the war effort. His mother dashed downstairs with Dan following. Once before, about a year ago, his father had called at Mrs. Swanson's apartment.

"Bobby? Bobby? Are you all right?"

Dan stood in the hallway of Mrs. Swanson's apartment, leaning forward to catch every word.

"Oh, thank God. Thank God you're well."

Then his mother stood silent, listening.

"I know. I love you, too. And I miss you. I miss you so bad."

She was going to cry. Dan knew it. He inched toward the stairway, not wanting to hear his mother cry.

After a five-minute wait his mother called out. "Hurry, Dan. Your father's in New York, but just for the night. He got lonely and wanted to talk to us. That was so sweet of him."

Dan picked up the phone.

"Hi, dad."

"Hello, Dan. How are you?"

The voice was so familiar. But though he tried, Dan was unable to attach a face--at least a current face--to the voice. Had his hair gotten grey? Had he grown a mustache or a beard? They spoke clumsily together, trying to recreate their father-and- son friendship. How was Dan doing in school? Was Dan playing baseball? Also they spoke quickly. Dan's father always worried about money, and this long distance phone call was chewing up his paycheck.

There was one question that burned in Dan's mind, that he had to ask somehow. In his last letter his father had said he unloaded his ship's supplies in a "new place." Was that "new place" a code word for France? Two months ago the Americans and the British landed off the coast of France in Normandy. It was D-Day, the biggest invasion of the war. All over the city churchbells rang and factory whistles blew. The next day newspapers printed huge headlines: WE INVADE!, ALLIES LAND IN FRANCE. Rules said you weren't supposed to talk to a sailor about his ports because a spy might be listening in on your conversation. But what if you asked kind of sideways?

"Dad, you said your ship unloaded in this new place. Well, we all know about D-Day, and I wondered ..."

"I got such a smart kid," said his father. "I'll bet I got the smartest kid in all Chicago."

He then changed the subject back to baseball, but Dan knew his hunch was right. His father's freighter now went directly to France instead of to England. This was a giant step closer to winning the war. Germany and the rotten Nazis are going down to defeat--and soon.

After a few more good-byes, the long-distance conversation ended. Dan went to Mrs. Swanson's kitchen, where his mother sat on a chair crying as if there had been a sudden death in the family. Her back was toward him. Mrs. Swanson bent over his mother, listening to her every sob.

"I just can't go on. I can't take it anymore," she said, her voice choking. "I want my husband. He's the man I married. I want him with me in my house."

"Yes, I know. This is terrible, this separation. It's no good, no fair."

Mrs. Swanson was at least twenty years older than Dan's mother. They were never close friends, but they always liked each other. Now, like a big sister, Mrs. Swanson searched the kitchen for something to dry tears. She found only a dishtowel.

"What am I doing, crying to you?" said Dan's mother. "You're all alone here, and ... and after all you lost." She then buried her face in the dishtowel.

Mrs. Swanson hugged her. "That's alright, Maria. Don't be ashamed to cry. These days there's no shame in crying. There's no shame at all."

Dan's mother turned and slowly withdrew the dishtowel from her face. Only now did she realize Dan had seen her crying. Her tears froze and her expression changed from sadness to rage.

"This darn war," she said.

"Yes," said Mrs. Swanson. "This darn war. This darn war."

Chapter Six

Monday morning and Dan, as usual, woke up to an empty apartment. His mother had dashed off to the Slave Brothers hours earlier. For Dan these were the lazy days of summer. School wouldn't start for two weeks. Today he'd go to the Logan Theater, find Tony standing in front, and the two would continue their quest to find the German spy ring on Lincoln Avenue. Spy-chasing was a silly way to spend a day, but at least it would keep Tony out of trouble. And besides, there had to be something fishy about that fellow Overcoat. No one kept a radio with a telegraph key in their apartment. With that radio old Overcoat could tap out code messages anywhere--even to the rotten Nazis in Germany.

At the front door Dan discovered a note:

Don't forget, Troop 242 is having its big scrap drive today. We've all got to meet at the American Legion Hall at 10:00 AM. See you there.

The letter was from Alfie Diaz. He signed it and even drew a Boy Scout medallion on top. Alfie was a patrol leader for Troop 242. Dan was assistant patrol leader. Alfie was chosen over Dan because ... well, because he was Goody-goody Alfie. Then Dan remembered he had vowed not to use that Goody-goody term any-more, not even in his thoughts.

What was Dan to do now? Tony was at this moment waiting for him at the Logan. Dan had for-gotten all about the Boy Scout scrap drive because scout meetings were irregular in the summer and this scrap drive was planned a month ago. Clearly meeting with the scouts was the responsible thing to do, and it would help the war effort. Tony never liked the scouts. Besides, the scout leader, old man Fanzone, said Tony was a troublemaker and wouldn't let him join the troop.

Dan decided he'd meet with the scouts this morning. It was right. It was a war-winning mission.

Thweeet. Thweeet.

Old man Fanzone loved to blow the scout leader's whistle he wore around his neck. He was a mailman who had a shiny bald head and was short. The boys joked he was so short that when he delivered the mail it took him three jumps to get letters in the slot.

Thweeet. Thweeet.

"Assemble right here, Troop 242. Right in front of me."

Dan stood in a military style formation. To his surprise, troops from distant neighborhoods were also assembled in front of the Legion Post. This scrap drive was a bigger deal than he'd imagined. One troop carried a huge, hand-lettered sign that said, COLLECT SCRAPS AND BEAT THE GERMANS AND THE JAPS. Even a guy from the regular Army was here, a major in a fancy dress uniform. He was overweight for a soldier and his belly bulged over his belt.

"Listen to me, scouts," said old man Fanzone. "That Army officer is going to talk to us. And when he says 'good morning, boys' he wants you all to shout as loud as you can, 'Good morning, sir!' That way you'll sound just like soldiers. Get it?"

The scouts all nodded.

"Good morning, boys," said the major.

"GOOD MORNING, SIR!"

The Major smiled and sucked in his large stomach.

"You boys, you're going to be soldiers today. You're soldiers who fight on the home front. We on the home front have to keep our men over-seas supplied with bullets and shells and bombs. That's what we do on these scrap drives."

He then went on to say the iron from one old frying pan could be made into a hand grenade, and that the blade of an old shovel could be melted down and turned into a bayonet. The scouts had heard similar speeches in earlier scrap drives.

"Yes, boys, we on the home front have to be just as alert and as diligent as the fighting men. Sometimes we're criticized, or at least I'm criti-cized, for not being over there in the foxholes and all. But I'm doing my duty organizing these scrap drives even though I'm not over there ... in the ... in the holes and all. So, boys, today we are going to go down the alleys looking for valu-able junk. Pick up anything--tin cans, old leather shoes, newspapers--anything. Do your duty as home front soldiers, and by God you'll strike a blow against Hitler and Tojo and all those other international criminals."

One of the scout leaders shouted out, "Let's hear it for Major Henderson." Everyone clapped and cheered. The major shook his fist in the air, smiling at the applause.

Then Troop 242 marched off with Mr. Fanzone at its head.

"Come on, guys, let's sing our scrap drive song," said Mr. Fanzone. Alfie sang the loudest. You could hear his high- pitched voice above the others.

Collect scrap, scrap, scrap, and more
And our scrap will win the war.

Singing, they marched all the way to their assigned territory. There they split up into patrols and searched the alleys and streets for war-winning trash.

"Nothin'. Can't find a thing," said a freckle-faced scout named Dick. "They've had too many scrap drives lately. All the good junk is gone from the empty lots."

It's true, thought Dan. Boy Scouts, Girl Scouts, YMCA, and church groups all held these drives in recent months. An all- girl organization called Little Orphan Annie's Jr. Commandoes had a scrap drive just last week. Those commandoes were good. The girls took all the prized stuff-- the loose tin cans, the occasional old tire, and the discarded buckets. All Troop 242 could find was some old newspapers and a piece of garden hose.

Alfie Diaz, who had been strangely silent, walked up to Dan. "We really don't have much stuff here, do we."

"No, but the other scrap drives took all the good stuff."

Alfie took off his glasses and rubbed them with the bottom of his scout shirt. "You know, I didn't sleep last night," he told Dan. "I mean, I went to bed, but then I couldn't sleep because I was worrying about what they're going to do to my dad in the Army."

"Hey, I told you, Alfie, maybe they won't even take him. And even if they do they'll keep him away from the fighting because of his bad feet."

"Bad back."

"Yeah, bad back, I forgot."

"My mother says she's worried sick. Me too. Worried sick."

"He'll be okay. He'll be okay," said Dan.

Dan's thoughts flashed back to that terrible day when an elderly Western Union man delivered a telegram to his landlady, Mrs. Swanson. It was a scene he tried to forget, but it kept haunting him. The telegram informed Mrs. Swanson that her son, Ernest, was killed in battle. For a long while Mrs. Swanson stood on the porch with the piece of paper in her hand, frozen like a statue. Sweat ran from her face in little rivers. Mr. Swanson stayed inside the apartment, peeking out at his wife from behind the shade. As far as Dan knew, he never came out of that apartment again. Six months later he died. Dan's mother claimed the poor man died of a broken heart.

Out on the street the nightmare of the telegram continued to unfold. After giving Mrs. Swanson her telegram the old Western Union man got on a bicycle. He still had more such telegrams to deliver. To Dan's surprise, about two dozen neighborhood people followed him. The old guy was pedaling his bike so slowly that the neighbors could walk and keep up with him. They all wanted to see where he would stop next. It was a curiosity, a morbid curiosity about what household would get the next telegram. In Dan's mind the messenger on his bike was the angel of death.

Thweeet. Thweet.

"Two-forty-two assemble over here."

The boys lined up in formation. Old man Fanzone looked down at the pitiful collection of scrap the troop had gathered.

"Two hours and that's all you boys found?" said the scout leader. "What the Sam Hill were you doing out here for two hours?"

"Some of the guys, they didn't want to work," said Alfie. "They've been horsing around and they … they forgot about the war effort."

All the boys stared hard at Alfie. What he said was a lie. Alfie was not only a snitch, he made up the stories he snitched about. But speaking out against Alfie always got Dan in trouble with

old man Fanzone. So he cursed Alfie silently-
-Goody-goody Alfie, he said in his mind. He
repeated the silent epithet over and over again:
Goody-goody Alfie. Goody-goody Alfie.

Chapter Seven

Where was Tony Avellini? For two straight mornings Dan waited for him where they always met outside the Logan Theater, but Tony never showed up. Dan knew that Tony hungered to go back to the Lincoln-Belmont neighborhood and snoop on the suspected spy ring. Now where was he?

There was only one thing to do, and that was to knock on Tony's door. Dan hadn't been to Tony's house in about two years. It wasn't that Tony's mother objected to Dan. In fact, Tony's mother always liked him. The problem was his own mother, who believed trouble followed Tony like a shadow.

Tony lived in a flat above a hardware store on Milwaukee Avenue. Dan found the store. Its front window was now covered with a gigantic victory poster that showed Marines charging off a landing craft over the words: BACK THE ATTACK: BUY BONDS. Dan went through the walkway and up the wooden stairs of the building's back porch. In the old days, when he used to go to Tony's place often, they always entered the back way.

Also, back in the old days, Tony used to come to Dan's house. Dan's mother liked Tony then. She thought he was funny. But Tony's life took a terrible turn. When he was nine years old, Tony's father ran off to California with a blond-haired woman. His dad had met the blond woman in church. In church! After his father ran away Tony started taking things and getting into trouble. Dan's mother said something snapped in poor Tony's head. Although she felt sorry for Tony, he was no longer invited into Dan's house.

Dan knocked on Tony's door. He knew his mother worked in a factory on the night shift, and he hoped he wouldn't wake her up. To his relief, Mrs. Avellini answered right away. She was his mother's age, but her hair was greying and wrinkles creased her face. At first she looked at him curiously. Then she smiled.

"Why it's Dan Zelinski, as I live and breathe. I haven't seen you in … in I don't know how long. My oh my, how you've grown."

Dan smiled. Adults always say that kind of stuff. He really hadn't grown very much at all, and that was another frustrating problem in his life.

"Is Tony home?"

Her face tightened. "Come in here a minute. Let me talk to you."

Dan entered the kitchen. The house smelled of cigarettes. In the next room he heard a bunch of ladies talking, and then he saw them sitting at the table playing cards.

"Now and then the girls come over and play gin rummy after work," Mrs. Avellini explained. "It's good for us. It gives us a way to relax."

Dan noticed that one of the card players was a colored lady. He was surprised by this. He'd never seen white people and colored people in a house playing cards together.

"I got to tell you about Tony," said Mrs. Avellini. She looked over at the card players and spoke in a half whisper. "Tony is ... Well, they locked him up."

"Jail?"

"Not so loud!"

"Sorry," said Dan.

"I think they're going to let him out tonight. I've got his bail money. Anyway, I'm going down there and I hope to pick him up. '

"What did he ..."

"I'll let him tell you the details." Mrs. Avellini lit a cigarette. "Dan, I know you two hang out together, and I know your mother disapproves of my boy."

"But she used to like him," Dan said, which was true.

"You're a good kid, Dan, and you're a good influence on my Tony." She closed her eyes, and squeezed them shut for a moment. "It's that rotten father of his. If he were here he could help me, but no. That good-for-nothing Dago, he ... he ... Oh don't get me started."

Dan bowed his head, not knowing what to say.

"He's a good kid at heart, Tony is, don't you think so?"

"Yes, I think he's very good at heart" said Dan. He was silent for a long moment, and then he announced, "I'd better be going now."

"Okay, bye, Dan," said Mrs. Avellini.

Then Dan waved inside to the ladies at the card table. "Good-bye."

"Bye-bye," came a chorus.

"Bye now, honeychild," said the colored lady.

What an odd thing to say. Honeychild? That sounded more like what a movie colored woman would say rather than a real live colored lady. But how would he know? He'd never talked to a colored lady other than the one who worked in the laundry on Kedzie Avenue, and with her they only talked laundry stuff.

The next morning Tony and Dan met in front of the Logan theater.

"Boy, am I glad to be out of that place," said Tony.

"Did they put you back in ... in The School?"

"Naaa, this time they had me in jail, a real jail. I mean I was in there with the men. Once I was in a cell with a guy who'd been in the Army, but they kicked him out."

"Why did they kick him out?"

"He told me he punched his sergeant. Then … then, after they kicked him out, he said he killed a guy. But maybe he was just making that part up."

"You mean people in there would brag about killing someone, even if they didn't really do it?"

"Crazy guys in that jail, real crazy."

Dan looked at Tony eye to eye. "What was it this time?" He surprised himself because his voice was suddenly so stern.

"What do you mean?"

"How did you end up in jail this time?"

"Oh, that."

"Yeah, that."

Tony stuffed his hands into his pockets. "You know, I took things. Nothin' big, just a couple of things from a real big store. I figured the store wouldn't miss them things. They got plenty of stuff there."

"What little things?"

"Ahhh, a few things. One … one radio."

"A radio!" Dan exploded. "That's an expensive one thing."

"It was just a little radio, the littlest one on the shelf. Then this guy in a suit grabbed me. He held me by the hair, the crumb. That's no fair, holding me by the hair. He snuck up on me. If I'd seen him first, he'd never catch me."

"A radio," Dan said with a sigh.

"Yeah, yeah, and a clock, too. I figured I could sell the clock. And an iron, I figured I'd give that to my ma."

"Wow!"

"So then I was three days in the jail. My mother came and paid bail money. And then a judge let me go. It was a woman judge. You ever seen a lady judge?"

"No."

But of course Dan had never seen a real live judge before. All the judges he'd seen were in the movies.

"What was the judge's name?" asked Dan

"I don't know. Just a woman, that's all. Real old she was, white hair and all. Anyway, she let me out, but sort of like on trial. Know what I mean?"

In Dan's thoughts he saw Tony being led away to a big prison and a stern-faced guard closing a huge iron door behind him. Dan became so afraid that he decided to take his mind off his worries by writing a movie, this one about a woman judge.

"Can't you remember anything about the judge's name?" asked Dan.

"No, just a woman, that's all. But you know, I think she liked me. That's why she let me out."

Dan's movie judge would be named Abigail Ross. She lives in a nice neighborhood way north near the lake, a place where all the kids are polite and smile all the time like Goody-goody Alfie does. Then she becomes a judge and has to deal with tough boys from the slums like Tony Avellini.

"What happens to you now?" Dan asked.

"Now I got to go back and see this judge in six months or something. I can't do nothin' bad like, well, take stuff. And she told me I had to do good stuff, too. I have to do what you Boy Scouts say, you know, the good deeds."

"Good deeds. Right, that's the Boy Scouts pledge."

"Yeah, that's it. And you know what?" He smiled for the first time. It was a bright smile, a smile that said he was bursting with fresh ideas.

"What?"

"I'm going to do the goodest good deed ever." The smile flashed like fireworks in the night. "I'm going to catch me them German spies."

Chapter Eight

They walked toward Lincoln Avenue, and this time Tony did not even ask if Dan had streetcar money in his pocket. Tony was on a mission. Dan felt as if the both of them were soldiers marching into battle.

After a furious walk, they stood outside of the tavern called the Hofbrau House. It was only ten in the morning, but the place was crowded with night shift men and women who had just gotten off work. Music from the jukebox drifted out of the open door.

"Nobody around here today," said Tony, "not Overcoat, not Thomas, not nobody."

Tony looked up at the second floor apartment.

"Back when I was in The School I knew a guy named Rocky. We called him Rocko because he was kind of crazy, you know, rocks in his head. He used to brag that his father was the best burglar on the North Side. This guy Rocko said his old man taught him all kinds of tricks, and then he told me some of them tricks."

Dan sensed trouble brewing in Tony's thoughts. "I hope you're not thinking what I think you're thinking."

"I'm not thinking nothing. I just want to see what the back of this place looks like, that's all."

Dan struggled with his feelings, knowing mischief was working in Tony's mind. The two walked around the block and looked at the building from the alleyway. They knew it was the back of the tavern because they could still hear the jukebox music.

"Fire escapes are sure funny things," said Tony looking up at the fire escape stairs and the platform along the building's alley side. "They let people out if there's a fire, but they let people in, too. That's what Rocko said he learned from his dad."

"Don't even think about it!" said Dan.

"Think about what?"

"What you're thinking."

"I was just thinking about looking through the window up there. Maybe we'd see some spy stuff."

"You want to go back to jail or what?"

"Hey, I'm going to catch me those spies. That old woman judge, she'll love me when I tell her about the German spies here."

When Tony was this determined to do something crazy, Dan was powerless to stop him. Now all he could do was hang around and try to prevent him from getting into a real serious fix.

Tony grasped his hands together and held them near his belt buckle, creating a step. "C'mon, you climb up and get them fire escape stairs down."

Behind Tony was a set of bars that guarded a long, narrow window. Near the top of the bars the stairs of the fire escape jutted outward.

"You can make it easy, and then grab them stairs and pull them down," said Tony, still making a step with his hands.

Dan was a good climber, and the bars were a challenge he could not resist. Besides, if the cops caught them climbing on a fire escape, it might not be so bad. At least they hadn't committed a burglary. Not yet anyway.

"Here I come," said Dan.

Taking a high step, Dan put his foot on Tony's hands. Then he felt Tony's brute strength lifting him upwards. In all their years together, the two had never had a fight. They had not even playfully wrestled. Tony said he lost his temper too easily to engage in any such horseplay. Now Dan was grateful of that. Tony was strong enough to be a champion weightlifter.

Dan scrambled up to the top of the bars and reached backwards with one hand to grab the main beam of the fire escape stairs.

"That's it," said Tony from below. "Pull them down and I'll catch them. Them stairs, they go real easy."

Dan tugged downward. Tony was right, it was easy. The stairs slanted down with a long, metallic squeak. Dan gave the railing a kick with his free foot, and the stairs inched low enough for Tony to grab them.

"See, I told you it was easy," said Tony.

Tony raced up the stairs. Dan climbed on and followed him.

Near the top, Tony announced, "Now wait. We got to let these stairs up smooth so we don't make a lot of noise."

With that Tony got off the last step and waited while the counterweight returned the iron stairs to the horizontal position. At the last minute Tony put his foot on the top step to slow the ascent and to muffle any clanging of metal to metal.

"See, smooth, huh?" he said with pride in his voice.

Right, smooth, thought Dan. He got the feeling Tony had sneaked up fire escapes many times before.

Tony and Dan tiptoed along the fire escape platform towards a door and a wide window. The building was only two stories high, so this upper apartment had to belong to Overcoat and Thomas. From the tavern below Dan heard jukebox music booming.

At the window Tony dropped to his hands and knees and crawled under the sill, so as to be unseen by anyone inside. Dan did the same. The window was half open and there was no screen. Pink and red curtains flapped outside in the breeze. Dan was strangely unafraid. They were only playing on a fire escape, a foolish but, he reasoned, not a terribly illegal activity. If a cop spotted them he'd say they were engaged in a new type of hide-and-seek game. But what if Overcoat popped out of the window with a gun in his hand? What then? He'd think about that later.

When they were both crouched under the window, Tony slowly raised his head to peek inside. After a second, Tony put his finger to his lips: "Shhhh." With his other hand he motioned Dan to take a peek.

Dan looked.

Inside was a scene stranger and more fantastic than any movie Dan had ever written. Along the wall of the apartment stood an elaborate radio outfit composed of a transmitter, a receiver, and a half dozen different meters. Dan recognized the equipment because last summer he'd studied to get a radio merit badge with the scouts. Sitting in the middle of a table, surrounded by the radio gear, was old Overcoat. He faced the wall with his back towards the window so he could not see Dan or Tony. Overcoat wore a set of earphones, and his right hand was on a telegraph key.

My God, thought Dan. He's sending messages to someone. Why, that old devil. He's giving vital information to submarines, and spies, and saboteurs. Right now he's planning to blow up factories, maybe even the one where his mother worked.

The jukebox in the tavern below blasted out "The Beer Barrel Polka," a lively song Dan had heard many times at weddings and at neighborhood block parties.

Dan gave another peek inside. The old man, his back toward the window, tapped diligently on the telegraph key. Suddenly he stopped and banged his fist on the table in an angry way. He no doubt was mad because he lost his radio signal. Dan thought, well what can you expect, you evil spy, Berlin is a long way from Chicago, you know.

Dan felt Tony touch him on the shoulder. Tony pointed towards the fire escape stairs, indicating it was time to go. Dan stuck one finger in front of his nose to show he'd leave in just a minute. Then he crawled past Tony towards the fire escape ladder that led to the roof. He pondered how strange it was that he and Tony were in a dangerous spot on a fire escape and this time it was he who wanted to delay their getaway.

Quietly Dan climbed the ladder until he could see the roof. There, as he suspected, was a long-distance radio antenna. Wires of the antenna stretched over the length of the roof to resemble a giant letter H. Dan had seen that type of antenna in the radio book he had taken out of the library. Alfie Diaz studied the book, too. Dan never finished the radio book because he spent too much time fooling around with Tony last summer. Of course, Alfie studied and he got the merit badge.

Something was odd about this antenna, though. To be efficient, it should be mounted on poles maybe ten, fifteen feet tall. But this antenna was only knee-high off the roof. Why would anyone build their antenna so low? There was only one answer to that question. Whoever put up that antenna did not want it to be seen from the street or from the alley.

Like a commando in the movies, Dan slipped down the ladder, ducked, and crawled to Tony at the fire escape stairs. The music below never stopped.

"Now there ain't no way to let these things down quiet," Tony whispered while pointing at the fire escape stairs. "So we just got to get on them stairs, let them hit the ground, and take off and run."

Dan nodded. Grasping the rail, Tony walked out--two steps, three steps, four. The stairs plunged and the end struck the concrete alley with a clang and a bounce. Tony and Dan rushed down. Like thieves on the lam, they raced through the alley towards the street. Perhaps Overcoat heard the clatter and was now aiming a high-powered rifle out the window. Dan could almost feel the crosshairs of the rifle's sight on his back. He never looked behind him.

They ran three blocks down Lincoln Avenue, five blocks down a side street, and they finally stopped at the big intersection of Lincoln, Belmont, and Ashland. There they stood with their hands on their knees, panting, listening to their hearts thump like drumbeats.

A whirlwind of thoughts stormed through Dan. Overcoat was a spy. But maybe Overcoat was just a guy who liked to tinker with radios. Then why the secret antenna? No, there was something strange, something unholy going on in that apartment above the tavern. For all Dan knew, old Overcoat was on that radio tapping out messages to Adolf Hitler himself.

Chapter Nine

Their walk back was silent. Spy? Secret agent? Saboteur? Those words and the sinister deeds connected with them hammered at Dan. What if they didn't turn Overcoat in to the police, and he blew up a factory or sank a ship? Then the deaths of all those sailors--men like his father--and all those factory workers--women like his mother--would be on his conscience.

"We got to go back to where Overcoat lives," said Tony. "Then we got to sneak in there and get some of that radio stuff. See, we take the stuff to the cops. They'll go put Overcoat in jail. Then we'll be ... we'll be, what do you call the good guys, real good guys."

"Heroes?"

"Yeah, heroes. And then that judge lady, she'll love me, and she'll tell me I never have to go back to the jail again."

"Yes," said Dan. "Judge Abigail Ross will be very happy with you."

"What? Who?"

"Nothing. I was just thinking out loud."

What a great ending for Dan's movie: The Italian boy catches the spies and helps win the war. The final scene shows a parade with marching soldiers and a band. Abigail Ross and the Italian kid are sitting in an open-top convertible riding down the street. Also in the car is the mayor of Chicago and a top-ranking Army general like MacArthur or someone. Wildly cheering people shower them with confetti. At last Dan had dreamed up a keen way to end one of his movies, but now he couldn't develop the idea. He was too occupied thinking about the spies.

"We got to go back there tomorrow," Tony said. There was fire in his voice. "We got to get into that place."

Dan couldn't say no to that plan. This time Tony, in his fantasy world, had stumbled upon the truth. Maybe the entire war effort hinged on what he and Tony did next.

"See you tomorrow," Tony said.

Dan nodded, knowing he would meet Tony in the morning no matter what.

It was after six o'clock when Dan got home. His mother was still at work. Apparently she had raced home for lunch because she left him a bowl of corn beef hash in the oven and a note telling him how to heat it up. Dan was too troubled to eat. He wondered if he should go to the police. No, they would just laugh at his spy story. Maybe he should talk with a man like the scout leader, Mr. Fanzone. Or he ought to report the spy to Mr. Schneider, Wisner Street's Air Raid Warden. But old man Schneider was a German, and maybe he too was taking orders from Hitler. Certainly he couldn't tell his mother what he'd seen. She'd be upset that he even spent a minute with Tony Avellini, much less whole afternoons.

Dan left the house and walked to Meyer's Drugstore to buy a candy bar. The candy would serve as his supper, even though his mother would get mad if she knew this. He opened the drugstore door, and the victory poster with the drowning sailor stood before him screaming out the message: SOMEONE TALKED! Dan's hunger vanished. He thought about his father and the icy waters of the Atlantic and the submarines and the spies. He had to do something now! Inaction just allowed Overcoat and the spies more time to complete their evil plans.

A bold idea burst into Dan's thoughts. He'd take the streetcar back to Overcoat's house and scout the place out himself. Maybe he could find out more information if he were alone, without Tony.

He said a quick prayer to his guardian angel, "Oh, dear Guardian Angel, watch over me in what I'm attempting to do tonight." That angel, he knew, had two functions. First he was a protector, but second, he reported all of Dan's secret sins directly to God. Was this angel truly his guardian? Or was he nothing but a dirty squealer?

Dan walked toward Belmont Avenue. He'd gone only one block when he met Alfie Diaz.

"Hi, Dan. How's tricks?"

Why did Alfie say that "How's tricks?" greeting? His father used to say that now and then, but Dan never heard a kid use the expression.

"I'm not up to any tricks," said Dan.

Alfie didn't catch the anger in Dan's voice.

"My father went away yesterday," Alfie said. "They sent him to some Army base in Missouri." He looked down and slowly shook his head. "Now I'm going to worry. Pretty soon they're going to send him overseas to fight, you watch."

Dan's anger melted away. He and Alfie now had a common bond. They both had fathers who could be killed in the war.

"Look, Alfie, I told you, your father is a taxi-cab driver, right? So the Army, they'll make him drive a jeep or a truck or something."

The memory of Tony's Uncle George stabbed at Dan. Uncle George also had a "safe" job driving a truck. Then, in North Africa, his truck hit a land mine and … .

"I got this funny feeling that I'm never going to see Dad again. I told you about this girl I know whose brother got killed in the war. She was a real nice girl, too. Now she cries all the time. Neighbors say she cries day and night. She can't stop crying. Can't stop."

Alfie sounded like he was choking. Dan wondered if he would break out in tears. "How about you?" he said in a voice just above a whisper. "Do you ever get funny feelings about your father out on that ship?"

"I don't let myself think about that," said Dan.

That was a lie. Every day he thought of his father and the hazards he faced at sea. Especially he could not forget seeing the old bicycle messenger drop off the telegram at the Swanson house. No matter how hard he tried to erase that scene from his mind, he still saw the neighbors following the old man down the street to see who would get the next telegram, the next terrible message.

They stood silent for a long moment, both locked in worries about faraway fathers. Finally Alfie broke the silence.

"Say, where are you going tonight?"

Dan couldn't tell him his mission. He couldn't tell anyone.

"I got some business, real important business to take care of," said Dan.

"Oh, yeah," said Alfie. "That sounds like … like mysterious stuff. Can I go with you?"

"No, no, this is something I got to do alone. All alone."

Dan left Alfie gazing after him with wonder. He'd never guess that Dan was going to Lincoln Avenue to spy on a bunch of spies.

At Belmont, Dan boarded an eastbound streetcar. He paid half fare and the conductor hardly gave him a second look. He cursed the fact that he could get on for half fare with such absurd ease. When would he ever grow up and look more like a man? At the rate Dan was going, he could probably get away with paying half fare even when he was fourteen, fifteen, maybe even at age eighteen! Perhaps the war would last until he turned eighteen, and it would be his turn to become a soldier. But then the Army would reject him because he still looked like a little kid. How embarrassing.

The streetcar was crowded. Dan found a seat in the back and gazed at the tired-looking men and women returning home from a long day's work. The lady in front of him no doubt toiled in a factory. She tried to fix her hair and look pretty even though her shirt was covered with grease from some machine. Maybe she made the parts that went into machine guns. Good job, Lady, Dan said in his thoughts. Keep up the great work for the war effort, and don't worry-- your hair looks just fine. Across the aisle sat a man wearing a business suit. He was so tired he dozed off while reading a newspaper. That guy, Dan imagined, was an engineer who designed the powerful, long-range bombers that now pounded German and Japanese cities. Way to go, Mister. Enjoy your nap.

A refreshing breeze flowed in from the street-car's open windows. Dan let the breeze wash over him, realizing this is why he liked street-cars so much. Buses were stuffy, and he always got sick on them. He hated to admit that because only little kids were allowed to get sick in buses and cars. Cars? There had never been a car in his family. He'd only ridden in cars a dozen or so times in his life. And he got sick in them, too.

At the intersection of Lincoln, Belmont, and Ashland, Dan got off and walked down Lincoln Avenue. Near the Hofbrau House tavern, he crossed the street to observe the upstairs apartment from the other side. He guessed that's what a proper counterspy would do. It was getting dark, but no lights were on in the apartment above the tavern. Old Overcoat was probably working the radio in the dark and plotting with his German comrades to sabotage the American war effort. What evil things was the old man up to tonight? Maybe he'd poison Lake Michigan, kill all the workers, and shut down every factory in Chicago.

From the tavern the jukebox played the same song as before. Some beer-drinker must have loved the "Beer Barrel Polka."

Wild thoughts whirled in Dan's mind. He wondered if Overcoat had secret pictures of Hitler and a swastika up there. Sure he did, and at night he got down on his knees and worshiped those pictures instead of saying prayers before a cross. He'd go to hell, that wicked old man. But spies are tricky. Probably Overcoat kept his swastika and Hitler pictures hidden. Maybe he even had a cross over his bed so guests would think he was a good Christian instead of a Nazi. Crafty guys, these spies.

Wait! Did Overcoat have a rifle that was right now poking out of a secret gunport and focusing in on his heart? What if Dan were shot and killed by that no-good Nazi spy right here on Lincoln Avenue? The old Western Union man, the messenger of death, would pedal up to his house and hand his mother a telegram.

Dan wrote a movie, the scariest one he ever made up. It took place in olden times in a little European village. An old man dressed in a black overcoat enters the village and rides a big white horse slowly down its main street. Death will come to any house where he decides to stop. All the peasants follow him in a solemn procession. They don't want to follow, but they can't turn their heads from this fallen angel. So they trail after him as if hypnotized by a terrible yearning to know which house he will visit next.

He'd better go home. Just thinking about the strange movie made him shiver. Of course, if he were a true patriot he'd stay here all night to see what suspicious-looking characters came and went from the apartment. But, darn it, being a counter-spy was a humdrum business. It was boring.

"Beer barrel. Beer barrel."

Who was that? Someone was chanting out words, not quite singing them.

Standing on Dan's right was Thomas, the strange kid. How does he do it? How does this guy just pop up next to you without you even knowing where he's coming from? He's like an elf in the cartoons.

"Beer barrel. Beer barrel. Nice song," said Thomas while pointing toward the tavern

"How did you get here?" asked Dan.

"How did you get here?" said Thomas, emphasizing the "you."

That was a good question, thought Dan. After all, he was the stranger in this neighborhood.

Dan said, "Well, I ... I took the streetcar to get over here."

"Streetcars. Nice. Don't have to walk. Don't have to walk."

Dan fumbled with his hands in front of him, not knowing how to start a conversation with this boy. Finally he said, "So, Thomas, how's tricks?" He could have kicked himself for saying that.

"Where's your friend?" asked Thomas.

"You mean Tony?

"Tony, Tony, Tony," said Thomas.

"Tony's at home, I guess."

"I like your friend. He's more fun than you. More fun."

Dan wasn't offended by that remark. Thomas meant it matter- of-factly, without insult.

"Say, Thomas," said Dan, trying to lead the conversation. "Let me ask you about that guy you live with."

"You mean him," said Thomas, turning his head and rolling his eyes towards the upstairs apartment.

"Yeah, him." Dan repeated, also turning and gazing at the place. "He talks like this on the radio," Dan made a motion with his hand as if he were working a telegraph key.

"Radio," Thomas said while imitating Dan's telegraph sign. He grinned, and once more Dan noticed his missing teeth.

"Who does he talk to?"

"Faraway. Real faraway."

"They're faraway, huh? Are they bad guys? I mean the faraway guys?"

Then Thomas laughed. "I don't want to talk to you because you no fun. Bring your friend. Talk to him good."

"Sure, Thomas. I'll bring my friend here tomorrow. Will you be here?

Thomas stared at him with a dreamy look, as if he had just slipped away into a trance.

"Yeah, right here. I'll bring Tony tomorrow in the morning."

Again the empty stare.

Forget it, Dan told himself. He'd bring Tony in the morning and just hope for the best. He left Thomas still listening to the music and chanting, "Beer barrel. Beer barrel."

Chapter Ten

"Ya mean you went down there to that Hof place without me?"

"Yeah, I figured I'd kind of snoop around and see what I could see. Then I ran into that nutty guy, Thomas. He said he'd be there in front of his place today."

They met, as usual, in front of the Logan Theater. At first Dan thought Tony would be mad at him for going to the spy's house alone, but that was not the case.

"Hey, maybe this will be easier than I thought." Tony was excited now and started walking around in little circles. "If Thomas lets us in the house we can grab some of that spy stuff and take it right over to the cops. Oh boy, the judge lady is going to love me for this. I'll never have to go back to another jail, not ever."

Dan's movie judge, the Honorable Abigail Ross, would call the whole Chicago police force out and have the cops stand at attention while she pinned a hero's badge on the spy-catcher's shirt. The scene flashed in Dan's mind--a band playing triumphant music, all the cops saluting at once. What a glorious movie this will be.

They took the streetcar at Belmont, paying two half fares. This time the streetcar was crowded and the conductor collected their fourteen cents without comment. Naturally, they used Dan's money.

Riding toward Lincoln Avenue, Dan felt a curious mixture of resolution and fear. He was now convinced something wicked was festering in the apartment above the Hofbrau House tavern. Whatever it was, it had to be reported to the authorities before a disaster happened that would reverse the course of the war. But what if Overcoat has a couple of Nazi storm troopers living with him? Those guys would torture them using all the awful Nazi torture methods he'd seen in the movies. Dan drowned his fears, knowing he had to do his duty. A deep feeling of determination overcame him despite the hazards he faced. Was this the way soldiers felt when they were about to go into battle?

"How long have we been here?"

"I don't know, an hour maybe."

Tony was getting impatient. They stood across the street from the Hofbrau House, every now and then eyeing the upstairs apartment. For a change no music came from the tavern's jukebox. Thomas was nowhere.

"Thomas said he'd be here, huh?"

"That's what he told me."

But where was the little guy? Maybe they should just go home and try this again another day. The grim devotion to duty Dan felt moments ago had faded. He shivered even though it was a warm morning in August.

"Think the cops already got them?" asked Tony.

"I doubt it. Old Overcoat is pretty secretive. We were lucky to find out what we did about him."

Dan wished he could stop shivering. He was afraid his teeth would start chattering. In his daydreams he imagined himself a heroic soldier, like the ones in the movies who stormed out on the battlefield and won the war single-handedly. Why was he so afraid now?

"We better find them soon," said Tony.

Suddenly the downstairs door cracked open. Without exchanging a word both Tony and Dan ducked behind a parked car. Tony was first to raise his head and peek over the car's hood.

"It's okay," said Tony. "It's Thomas and he's alone. He's just standing in front of the door. He's not even looking our way. Let's cross the street, He won't even know we been hiding behind this car."

They crossed. When Thomas saw Tony he broke into a cracked-tooth grin.

"Hi, Tom, hi," said Tony.

Thomas's grin grew even wider.

"Hey, Tom, my friend says he saw you the other day and that you wanted to talk to us."

"Talk to you," Thomas said, pointing to Tony. "You're more fun than friend."

"Lookit, what if we talked upstairs in your house?" Tony asked.

"Can't do that." Thomas swung his head, looking upstairs toward the apartment window above the tavern. "He don't like that. He says nobody come up to house. Nobody, nobody, nobody, not nobody."

Tony also looked up towards the apartment. "Is ... is he home now?"

"No, not home now."

"Then let's go up there. He'll never know."

"He tell me nobody, nobody, not nobody ever."

"Look it, is he a good guy?"

"Yes." Then he looked down at his feet. "Sometimes not so good."

Dan was happy to be removed from this conversation. Tony had a magical way of talking to Thomas. If Dan tried to say anything the guy would just go into his dreamy mood.

"Is he bad, the man you live with?"

Thomas said nothing. But in Tony's mind, Thomas had just agreed that Overcoat was a bad guy.

"So, look, you don't have to do what a bad man tells you to do. I have this friend who's a judge, a woman judge. You know what a judge does?"

Thomas nodded his head as if to say yes.

"Right, a judge puts you in jail if you're bad. But this lady I know is real good. So I do whatever she tells me to do. But if she was bad I wouldn't do what she wanted. I'd do just the opposite. See what I mean?"

Dan suddenly had a new vision. In his movie Judge Abigail's ghostlike figure rises over the slum kid's head in a cloud of pure white smoke. She'd be a guardian angel. Abigail the angel would whisper in the kid's ear reminding him to do good deeds like catching spies. That's it! Dan would write a fantasy. His heroic woman judge would float above the movie character the way a spirit floats above a person. Only the heroic kid could see her. Every time she made an appearance the audience would hear sweet music in the background. This movie would certainly win the Academy Award.

Finally Thomas spoke. "Alllll right, let's go my house." Again he grinned, exposing his missing teeth. Dan did not want to get too close to him. He probably never brushed and his breath smelled bad.

Thomas turned around and grasped a key that hung from a string around his neck.

"Got my key on a string. Funny?"

Tony chuckled, as if he found the key thing to be hilarious.

The hallway was dark and the stairs squeaked under their feet. At the top of the stairs Thomas again fumbled with the key tied around his neck. Dan's fear had subsided and he no longer trembled. Sinister old Overcoat wasn't home. Besides, they were being invited into the apartment by Thomas. No one was breaking any laws. But what about the other Nazis that might live there? Dan chased the thought from his head.

Inside the apartment stood mountains of clutter. Boxes, books, and yellowed newspapers were piled high on the dining room table so that it was impossible to eat there. The newspapers were in a foreign language. The place smelled of cooked cabbage and of people who didn't bathe often. Facing the wall in the living room was a table that held radio equipment, the same equipment they had seen through the window yesterday. The radio area was the only neat-looking spot in the house. The rest was an unholy mess. That was what Dan's mother said when she was disgusted with the sight of his bedroom: "This room is an unholy mess!"

"Hey, look at all that nice radio stuff," said Tony, acting as if he were seeing the equipment for the first time. "Are you a radio man, Tom?"

"Radio stuff," said Thomas with a smile.

Tony pointed to the telegraph key in the middle of the desk. "Does ... does he talk on the radio a lot with this thing, this code thing?" said Tony. "You know who I mean, the guy who lives with you here."

Tony amazed Dan. Here they were in the house of a Nazi spy, they could be killed any minute by a stormtrooper, and Tony was calmly pumping information from this very odd boy who had to be connected to the spy ring. Maybe the FBI should hire Tony to be a super counterspy and catch every Nazi secret agent in the country.

"He talks," said Thomas pointing at the key.

"Now look, Tom, you want to help us with the bad guys, don't you?" said Tony.

"Yes."

"Okay. Remember that lady judge I told you about who's real good?"

Thomas nodded.

"Let us take a couple of these radio things to the judge. She'll see it's all bad stuff, and she'll come and get the bad guys here."

"He be mad!" Thomas almost jumped off his feet at the thought of someone taking the radio gear. "He be real mad."

"Look, I'll tell you what we'll do," said Tony. Slowly he crossed the room and opened the window. "See here. You got a fire escape right here. It'd be easy for some burglar to come in and take some radio stuff and then beat it out the window and down the fire escape. You can tell him a burglar took the radio stuff"

"He be real mad. Mad, mad, mad, mad, mad."

"Yeah, but he'll be mad at the burglar, not at you."

Thomas appeared to be puzzling out Tony's words in his mind.

"So my friend here," Tony pointed at Dan, "he knows a lot about radio stuff. He'll just take the wires off one of these things, and we'll take them to the woman judge." Tony motioned Dan over to the radio table. "This guy knows what he's doing around radios. Let him take care of the radio things."

Actually, Dan did not know what he was doing, but dismantling this equipment ought not to be a problem. Gingerly Dan traced the wire from the key to a chassis filled with vacuum tubes. He knew the key would be connected to the transmitter, and that was what they should take to the police. Suddenly the old song "Dry Bones" popped into his head: "Oh, the telegraph key's connected to the trans-mitter." Dan wondered why he thought of something so foolish. Taking this equipment to the police would break up a spy ring and save the world from Nazi conquest. Why should he think of the comic song "Dry Bones" at this historic moment?

Tony continued his soft conversation with Thomas, but Dan tried not to hear. Removing this transmitter was the most important thing he'd ever done in his life. He couldn't make a mistake. First he had to take the cord out of the wall socket. That was simple enough. Then he unfastened the wires to the key, also simple. Next he slid the transmitter towards him to reveal a half dozen wires attached to screws in the back. If he were a proper Boy Scout he'd "Be Prepared," and have a screwdriver in his back pocket. Goody-goody Alfie would have thought to bring a screwdriver if he were going to steal a spy's radio transmitter. Dan reached into his pocket and fingered a thin dime. That ought to work. Using the dime as a screwdriver, he detached wire after wire. He could almost see the fantasy figure of Abigail Ross rising above him and saying, "Ataboy, Dan, ataboy."

"You getting it?" Tony asked.

"Yeah, only one more screw."

At last Dan picked up the transmitter and showed it to Tony. The transmitter was just a little bigger than the table model radio set he had at home.

"Now remember, Thomas, burglars did this," Said Tony. "It was a burglar who came through the window and made off with the radio thing."

Thomas looked confused, but clearly he was not going to stop them from liberating the equipment.

"The police will be here soon," Tony said. "Maybe even the judge will come here too and give you a medal or something."

Yes, thought Dan. Her Honor Abigail Ross won't let you down, Thomas. Not good old Abigail.

Dan and Tony edged toward the front door. Dan held the transmitter in both hands.

"You sit tight, Thomas," Tony said. "We'll be back real soon."

Footsteps broke the stillness, heavy footsteps climbing stairs. They froze. A key twisted in the lock. The doorknob turned, and the door swung open.

Overcoat!

"Vat you do? You tief. You I kill!

Chapter Eleven

"The window," Tony shouted. "Make for the window!"

Tony ran and scrambled out the open window and onto the fire escape. He did this all in one move, as if he were diving into the pool at the YMCA.

Still carrying the transmitter in both hands, Dan rushed toward the window. Behind his back he heard Overcoat charging after him.

Tony was already on the fire escape landing. He reached through the open window and held out both hands. "Give me the radio thing," Tony shouted. "The radio."

"Radio. Radio. Radio. Radio," Thomas said.

He was giggling. The guy must have fallen back into his dream world.

Dan stretched out his arms to pass the transmitter through the window to Tony. Suddenly he felt an iron grip on his left shoulder. Overcoat!

"You stop. You I kill."

Overcoat's vicelike hand locked Dan's shoulder. He couldn't get away, but he managed to shift the transmitter to his other hand and hold it towards the window.

"Tony, take the transmitter," Dan shouted.

Tony grabbed the transmitter, set it down, and then seized Dan's hand. With all his amazing strength, Tony pulled.

"I ain't going to leave you here," said Tony.

Dan felt as if he were the rope in a tug-of-war contest, with Tony pulling one way and Overcoat the other.

"You I kill," said Overcoat again.

Now, thought Dan, was his moment to be a true American. Like a hero in Terry and the Pirates, he would sacrifice himself for the war effort. "Take the transmitter and get out of here," Dan yelled at Tony.

"No, I ain't leavin' you here," said Tony as he continued to tug at Dan's arm.

Overcoat, his face red with fury, shouted, "You tief. I call police."

An idea exploded in Dan's head. Yes, police. Surely this old man, this Nazi spy, wanted nothing to do with the police.

Dan blurted out, "Yeah, let's go get the police. Right now, let's go to the police station."

The redness drained from Overcoat's face.

"Who you?"

"Never you mind that. I said, let's go get the police."

Dan felt the old man's grip on his shoulder lighten.

"No. No police. You give me." He pointed to the transmitter. "Then you go. You get out."

"No! I know all about you and your spy friends," said Dan. He was now talking tough, but tough talk was the only thing a Nazi would understand. "We're going to the police with this stuff."

"Why police?"

"Because you're a spy. You're a spy for the Nazis and me and my pal are going to turn you in before you blow up a factory."

Overcoat smiled. It wasn't an evil smile. Instead the old guy looked as if he had just understood the punch line of a funny joke.

"Me spy?" He released Dan's arm and pointed to his chest with his thumb. "Me Nazi?" He then threw his hands into the air and laughed. "Me Nazi spy? Ha!" He laughed and laughed again, probably loud enough to be heard across the street.

"You come. You come in house. You both come. We talk."

Dan glanced at Tony and saw a puzzled look on his face. Slowly Tony stepped through the open window carrying the transmitter with him.

"You boys. You sit." Then he smiled again, and Dan saw that he was missing teeth too, just like Thomas. "Me Nazi? Me spy?" He laughed again. Then he shook his head and sighed. "Me, I tink Hitler, him jackass. Big Nazi jackass."

For a second Dan thought he noticed a hint of embarrassment in Overcoat's expression. Maybe he was ashamed that the house was in such an unholy mess. But after all he didn't expect guests. Especially he didn't think a couple of kids would sneak in, steal his transmitter, and accuse him of being an agent for Hitler.

Overcoat looked over at Thomas. "He let you inside?"

They both nodded.

The old man's voice grew angry. "He should know better."

"Don't blame him," said Tony. "We kinda … kinda tricked him into letting us in."

"I blame him for noting. He call me uncle. But I no uncle. He the son of my friend. He see too many bad things. Twelve years old and he already see bad things in war."

"He's seen the war?" Dan asked.

"Too much. Too much war." Overcoat then pointed to his own head as if to indicate Thomas was addled in his thinking.

"There's something wrong with him, huh?" Dan spoke in a whisper, but he was pretty sure Thomas could hear him.

"What you tink?" said Overcoat as if he resented the question. "He, what you say, confuse."

"Does he talk in German?" asked Tony.

"German ... No," said Overcoat, shaking his head slowly. "You young people, this country, you know nothing about language. He talk Polish language, just like me."

Overcoat was right. Dan was a typical American kid, and he knew so little about foreign languages he couldn't distinguish German from Polish. Dan repeated his vow to learn six languages after the war. He'd start with French. All smart people know French.

"I tell you story. You want hear story?" said Overcoat. "It sad story."

"Sure," said Dan.

"I work for his father in Poland," said Overcoat pointing at Thomas. "His father rich man. Own factory. Factory make typewriters. Then Nazis come Poland, take factory, make machine guns. His father escape. Go to Switzerland. But Thomas and mother no can escape. His father try to get Thomas and mother to Switzerland, too. Nazis find out. Take mother to jail. This boy," again he pointed to Thomas, "... he see all this. He see Nazi soldiers come to house, take mother, drag her out. Very bad. Very sad."

"What happened to the mother?" asked Tony.

"We don't know. No know nothing."

Dan looked over at Thomas who stood still as a statue. They were talking about the fate of his mother, but not paying any attention to him. Poor Thomas. Everyone dismisses him as if he were a piece of furniture.

"He saw all that, with his mother and all?" said Dan. Darn it, now he was doing the same thing, talking about Thomas like he wasn't even in the room.

"Yes. He see everyting." Overcoat talked in a voice so sad Dan thought he was about to cry. "That why he mix up. He smart boy. But see his mother and Nazi soldier … now he confuse. Too much. Too much war."

Dan tried not to stare at Thomas. He was the first true war casualty Dan had ever met.

"Now you," Overcoat stared at the two of them. "Why you tink I Nazi? Why you tink I spy?"

"Because you got that secret radio and the antenna on the roof," Dan said.

"How you know dat?" Overcoat snapped. "You spy. You spy on me."

"Well ... well, that's true," said Dan, knowing he was admitting an offense. "But we're fighters on the homefront. It's our duty to turn in spies."

"Look, radio antenna secret. But because I no have license to send the radio signals."

"We thought you were a German and you talk to Germany on that thing," Tony said.

"I no talk Germany. I talk Switzerland. I try. It is difficult for radio. I try talk to his father with radio. It is what you call illegal, but I talk anyway. I talk because ... because I love the boy and his father my friend."

Overcoat covered his face with his hands. Dan guessed he was weeping. And to think Dan believed he was a hard and cold Nazi agent.

"Then you ain't no Nazi," said Tony.

"Nazi," said Overcoat, spitting out the word. "I tell you something. This boy," once more he pointed to Thomas, "the boy Jewish. Mother and father Jewish. Nazi hate Jews. Nazi KILLING Jews in Europe." He shouted out the word killing. "You people, this country, no know this. Maybe after war you learn. Me, I Polish. I Catholic. I hate no one. I kill no one."

He sobbed. Genuine tears streamed down the old man's face. Dan wondered what to do. He had never seen a grown man cry before.

In a voice mixed with sobs, Overcoat said, "You boys, you Catholic?"

They both nodded, yes.

"Then you should know. Hate big sin, very big sin. I hate no one. You hate no one. No hate no one, then you good Catholic." Now he sobbed, even louder than before.

"How come you're in Chicago?" Dan asked. He had to say something to break this crying spell.

"My sister she live in Chicago. Then my sister, she get the pneumonia, she die."

Dan made a silent prayer: Oh, God, please don't let him start crying again.

"Why do you live in this neighborhood with all the Germans here?" said Tony.

"Not all German bad people. Man who own this building German. He feel sorry for me and Thomas. Give cheap rent. I work in tavern downstair. I sweep floor, clean window."

"There's plenty of jobs in the city," said Dan. "You can get a regular job in a factory or something?"

"Here I live like criminal," said Overcoat. He looked left and right as if expecting to find someone watching him. "I no have papers. My passport Poland. Police find me, they lock me up. If I go jail, who help Thomas?" Then Overcoat looked at his hands, studying them. "Beside, I no good work in factory. You know what work I do in Poland?" A sparkle came to his eyes. "I poet." He smiled, flashing his broken teeth. "What you tink dat? Poet. You believe?"

"I believe you, I guess," said Dan.

"You young. You believe many things. You good boy."

Finally Tony said, "I think we better just go and leave these guys alone."

"I think you're right," Dan agreed.

"You no tell police about radio, about me no papers?" Overcoat said.

"Don't worry I won't go to no cops," said Tony.

Dan made no such promise. With no papers and an illegal radio, Overcoat was breaking the law. It was Dan's duty as a home front soldier to report him.

Overcoat opened the front door. "This ... problem, his mother, his father, all because of war. War must end. No more war afterward, not ever."

"Right, no more wars," said Tony.

That's for certain, Dan thought. After this war, there would never be another one. Presidents and men in government will have learned how horrible wars are, and they would never get the country into one again.

As they left Tony turned to Thomas, "Hey, you're okay, Tom. I like you a lot."

"I like you," said Thomas. "You come back?"

"Sure, I'll see you again."

Out on the street, Tony said, "You know, those two are okay."

Dan, lost in conflicting thoughts, said, "I don't know. Maybe we should still go to the police."

"Why do we want the cops?"

"Because that guy Overcoat, he's here without papers. And he's got that radio, too. That's against the law."

"Wait a minute, calm down," said Tony. "Old Overcoat, he ain't hurting nobody. I don't care about his papers or his radio. Besides, remember what he said, what would happen to Thomas if Overcoat was locked up in jail?"

"Think of it this way," said Dan, deciding to appeal to Tony's selfish interests. "If you told the police about the old guy and they arrested him, then maybe the lady judge will say you're a hero and that you'd never have to go back to jail."

Tony pondered that possibility. "You know, I don't think that lady judge is like that. She'd probably get mad at me for turning in a nice guy, a guy who really ain't doing nothing bad."

Now it was Dan's turn to consider Tony's beliefs. His words rang with truth, like a church bell chiming on Sunday morning. Sometimes what seems wrong is right and what seems right is wrong. Dan had a lot of thinking to do.

As they walked Dan asked, "Will I see you tomorrow?"

"No 'cause I better see the lady judge. She told me to come up to her office, just drop in now and then."

"Say hello to Her Honor Abigail Ross for me," said Dan.

"What? That's not her name."

"I know. I'm just thinking out loud."

Suddenly Tony stopped walking and stood firmly on the sidewalk. He took a deep breath and said, "You know what I'm going to tell that judge tomorrow?"

"What's that?"

"I'm going to tell the judge lady that I quit taking stuff. And I mean what I'm saying." His face tightened with a look of grim determination. "You know, I don't take that stuff from stores because I need it. I take it because I'm mad. I'm mad at my dad and ... and what he did to me and my ma by running off with another woman. I'm mad at a lot of things. So I take stuff from stores."

This was amazing, thought Dan. Tony never talked about his theft problem before. He always denied it was an issue in his life. Dan wanted him to go a step farther.

"Steal. Say the word steal," said Dan.

"Why?"

"Because it's different than saying just taking stuff. You know, it sounds stronger. Besides, that's what it says in the Bible: 'Thou shalt not steal.'"

"All right, I'll say it. I ain't going to steal no more, not from the stores, not nothing. Stealing does you no good. It just gets you thrown in jail."

"That's right, Tony. I'll bet you're thinking now about Sister Theresa. Remember all the stuff she told us about sin and the fires of hell."

"Yeah, I remember that, but I'm not thinking about her now. I'm thinking of that kid, you know, Thomas."

"Thomas? Why Thomas?"

"I told you I steal because I'm mad, right?"

"Right."

"Well, look at that guy Thomas. He lost his home, he lost his country, and ... and maybe he even lost his mother. That's all because of the war. So he must be mighty mad. He's mad at the world, mad at a whole lot of things."

"Yeah, you're right. Thomas sure has a lot to be mad about."

"Thomas is madder than me and he doesn't go around stealing things and getting in trouble with the cops."

They both stood, not saying a word for a long moment.

"Is that what you're going to tell the judge lady tomorrow, that you're not going to steal anymore, not ever?" Dan asked.

"Yes."

And Dan was certain Tony would keep his word.

That Sunday morning Dan and his mother walked to church. It was late August, 1944. In a few days, school would start and Dan would enter the eighth grade. Of course, far more important events were rocking the earth. In Europe, Allied armies rolled over France and were poised to free Paris from the Germans. In the Pacific, the Americans conquered a Japanese-held island chain called the Marianas. Newspapers and radio announcers claimed American forces were victorious on both sides of the world. Still, nobody dared to predict when this bloody war would end. And it seemed that every month the number of American casualties were higher than the previous month. Every day a flood of telegrams came from the War Department to households on the home front. Families lived in mortal terror of telegrams.

Ahead, Dan spotted the Diaz family and hurried to catch up with them. It was Sunday, and he figured good Catholic neighbors should walk to Mass together.

"Hi, Alfie," said Dan, putting on his nice, Sunday voice. "Have you heard from your father yet?"

Alfie smiled. "We got a letter just yesterday. He says there's a real good chance he'll be stationed at some base in Wisconsin for the rest of the war. What do you think of that?"

"That's great. Wisconsin isn't far. You can go and visit him. You know, take the train."

"Right."

Dan changed the subject. He was still troubled about his failure to report Overcoat.

"Say, Alfie, I want to ask you a question, something I been wondering about. What if you knew someone was doing something that was against the law, but it really wasn't so bad. And if you told the police about him it would really hurt another person. What would you do? I mean, as a Boy Scout, what would you do?"

"I'd report the guy to the police," he said without hesitation. "The guy's breaking the law and the police should know about it. Besides, maybe they'd give me a reward or something."

"Yeah, I see."

Poor Alfie, thought Dan. He'll never understand that there's more to life than just getting another merit badge.

During the Mass Dan said a silent prayer, promising God that he would never report Overcoat to the police even though the man was breaking the law.

As they walked home from church, Dan's mother turned to him and grinned.

"I saw a real funny sign in Goldsmith's Meat Market yesterday."

Old man Goldsmith always had funny signs in his butcher shop. One sign said: "The Wurst You Get Here Is The Best."

"It was a war sign," said his mother. "You know how women are supposed to collect kitchen fats in tin cans and give them to the butcher?"

"Right," said Dan. "The butchers send the fats to factories where they make explosives for bombs and shells."

"Well, this sign was above the radiator, and it said, 'Ladies, Please Don't Put Your Fat Cans

On The Radiator.' Get it? Don't put your fat cans, you know, your fat behinds," she patted herself on the bottom, "on the radiator. Get it?"

Wow! This was shocking. Dan's mother never cracked a joke like that to him before. She never even hinted at something that might be just a little bit sexy or dirty when he was around. Now she stood giggling at her little story. Maybe this was her way of telling him he was growing up.

"What do you think would happen if your father saw that sign at Goldsmiths'?"

Dan thought, and said, "He'd probably laugh so hard he'd pee in his pants."

Dan's mother held her hand to her mouth trying to conceal a broad smile. Finally they both laughed together as they walked the next half block. Then Dan's mother thought of his father, and looked down at the sidewalk. Dan read her mind.

"This darn war," said Dan.

"This darn war," said his mother.

During World War II (1941-1945) the American government produced hundreds of "Victory Posters" which hung on the walls of schools, post office buildings, and factories. Usually the

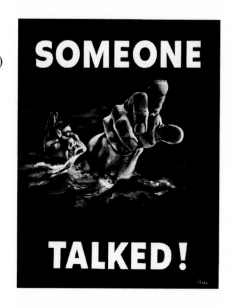

posters urged Americans to report to their jobs every day and work hard for victory. Some Victory Posters cautioned citizens to always be alert for spies.

The poster featured here, SOMEONE TALKED!, carried the message that some worker's loose talk was overheard by an enemy secret agent and resulted in an American ship being torpedoed by a submarine. One version of this poster showed a freighter sinking behind the drowning sailor. Victory Posters served as a constant reminder that America was at war with brutal enemies and therefore all citizens must act as soldiers.

I was born and grew up in Chicago. At eighteen I joined the Marine Corps. After my discharge I earned a degree in history from the University of Illinois.

Over the years I have published about 300 books for young readers, most of them factual history books. This novel, SOMEONE TALKED!, is based partially on my childhood. I was a kid during the World War II years (yes, I'm that old). I remember well the frenzies and fears of the wartime era.

I became a Chicago Cubs fan in 1945, the last year of the war and the last time the Cubs won the National League Pennant. The team has not won a World Series since 1908. Without doubt the Cubs have the most dismal record in baseball history. But we Cubs fans are an optimistic bunch. We live on hope.

—R. Conrad Stein

The World War II Home Front

R. Conrad Stein

DECEMBER 7, 1941, began as a normal Sunday in early winter. People went to church and looked forward to an afternoon of listening to football games on the radio. A bitter war raged in Europe, but the United States was not involved in that conflict. Americans generally believed they were isolated from foreign wars by the broad oceans on either side of their country.

Then, suddenly, the ordinary Sunday became a stunning day, one that altered the lives of all Americans. Radio programs were interrupted and excited voices announced that aircraft from the Empire of Japan had bombed the American navy base at Pearl Harbor, Hawaii. Upon hearing the news, many Americans cursed the Japanese. Some family groups fell to their knees and prayed. Still others looked at maps, not knowing exactly where this Pearl Harbor place was.

The next day President Roosevelt addressed Congress. He called December 7 "a date which will live in infamy." The president asked for and received a Declaration of War on Japan. On December 11 Germany and Italy declared war on the United States. With shocking swiftness the nation found itself in World War II, the largest and deadliest conflict in history. At its height some fifty nations representing more than half the world's population were involved in the war. The fighting raged until 1945. Estimates say at least fifty-five million people around the world died in combat or from hunger and disease brought on by the great clash of arms.

During the war years millions of American men and women served in the military. Those who did not enter the armed forces contributed to final victory by doing their part on what was called the home front. With hard work and patriotic zeal, the men and women at home poured their energies into an all-out effort to defeat the nation's enemies. The home front experience was unique in American history. Never before was the country so unified. The vast majority of Americans believed they were fighting evil enemies who would enslave them if given an opportunity.

President Roosevelt asked his countrymen to turn the nation into "the arsenal of democracy." This meant making weapons and munitions on a grand scale. Americans responded heroically to the president's challenge. Factories around the nation operated twenty-four hours a day as Americans manufactured 102,000 tanks, 2,500,000 trucks, and 300,000 aircraft. The country had just survived the Great Depression of the 1930s, when as many as one in four Americans suffered unemployment. Now everyone had a job and the factories sought all the additional hands they could find.

The war at home was a time of frustrations and worries. Yes, people had money in their pockets because of full employment. But there were fewer goods on store shelves. No one could buy a new car because car companies were devoted to making jeeps and trucks which were needed for the war effort. Food items such as butter and meat were rationed. Even the purchase of shoes was limited.

Concern for friends and relatives haunted people on the home front. Practically everyone had a cousin, an uncle, or a friend who served on faraway battlefields. In a front window, each household with a family member in the military displayed a special banner with a blue star. Those who lost a relative in battle showed a flag bearing a gold star. The gold star, the symbol of death, became a common sight as the war dragged on and casualties mounted.

The big letter V, for Victory, was seen everywhere on the home front. On windless days skywriting airplanes drew a giant letter V above a city and then put dot-dot-dash, Morse Code for V, under the letter. Write to a soldier or sailor and you sent the letter via Victory Mail or V Mail. Victory Posters hung in post offices and other public buildings urging people to work hard and not to take unnecessary days off from their factories. African Americans suffered discrimination at the time, so they adopted a symbol with a double V which stood for victory over the foreign enemy and victory over racial discrimination at home.

Popular music had a win-the-war theme. Songs such as "Coming in on a Wing and a Prayer" exalted American Air Force men. "Praise the Lord and Pass the Ammunition" invoked patriotism and suggested that God was on America's side during the conflict. The song "Der Fuehrer's Face" heaped ridicule upon America's principal enemy, Adolf Hitler. Many wartime tunes captured feelings of loneliness and distant love - "Don't Sit Under the Apple Tree (With Anyone Else But Me)," "You'd Be So Nice To Come Home To." Some songs scorning the Japanese were outwardly racist; one such song was titled "We're Gonna Have To Slap A Dirty Little Jap."

Hollywood entertainers and musicians joined to urge Americans to buy War Bonds. The War Bonds were paper notes signifying that the buyer had given the government a loan to be paid back later. The loan helped to finance the war effort. A common War Bond cost $18.75 (which was almost a week's pay for some workers) and was redeemable in ten years for $25.00. Children were asked to buy War Stamps for ten cents each. The stamps, similar to postage stamps, were stuck in a book called My Victory Book. When every page in the My Victory Book was filled with stamps the child exchanged the book for an $18.75 bond. The bonds and stamps were commonly called Victory Bonds and Victory Stamps.

Although the war was fought overseas, the nation prepared itself for possible attack. Entire cities shut down during air raid drills. Neither the Germans nor the Japanese had aircraft with the range to reach American shores, but the practice raids were still held. The drills took place at night and all households had to turn out their lights. Street lights were also extinguished. For obvious reasons, the air raid drills were commonly called blackouts. Such blackouts were useful in cities off the Atlantic coast where German submarines lurked, as the subs could spot ships in the background of city lights and torpedo the vessels.

Life for children changed dramatically during the war years. Adult supervision diminished because fathers and mothers were busy at work or away serving in the military. Thus children were on their own. Amazingly most of them avoided getting into big trouble. Toys were few because factories concentrated on churning out war goods. Consequently children played imaginary games without toys. Even the made-up games had a war theme. "Let's play guns," boys would say. Language altered for the age-old game of hide-and-seek. When one kid tagged another the words "you're it" now became "you're captured."

Hunting down enemy spies and saboteurs was a thrilling activity for kids, one that allowed them - in their minds, at least - to contribute to the war effort. The government indicated that spies operated everywhere. Victory Posters issued by the government said LOOSE LIPS SINK SHIPS, warning people not to talk about the work they did in war goods factories because a saboteur might overhear their idle chatter. A particularly scary poster showed a drowning sailor and the words SOMEONE TALKED! The poster implied that a dock worker talked about the ship he loaded and unleashed a tragic chain of events. The dock worker's loose talk was heard by a spy, the spy informed a submarine through a secret radio, the sub torpedoed the ship and cast the sailor into the sea.

Was this effort to defeat enemy secret agents warranted? No doubt spies operated in the United States, but we know little about them because they kept their activities under tight wraps. Saboteurs, those who wished to destroy key wartime facilities, were another matter.

On a night in May of 1942 German submarines surfaced and two rubber crafts bearing eight men paddled to shore. The eight Germans had lived in America, and they spoke flawless English. They wore American style clothes and they had dollars, issued by the German government, in their pockets. The eight were saboteurs. The men had been sent on a special mission to blow up American power plants. Among the weapons they carried were several bombs disguised as lumps of coal. If one of those innocent-looking lumps were shoveled into a boiler driving a generator, the boiler would explode cutting off electrical power for many factories and offices. Despite careful planning, events went awry for the saboteurs almost immediately. Several were caught by the Coast Guard on Long Island in New York State soon after they left their submarine. Others were apprehended as they scattered throughout the country. One man was arrested in a New York City tavern where he was spending his German-issued American money on beer.

As far as is known, this effort by eight rather clumsy German agents was the only attempt at sabotage ever launched by the enemy during World War II. Still, wartime Americans saw spies and saboteurs lurking everywhere. Radio dramas and movies told stories of alert citizens who helped round up these dangerous enemies. Children were especially excited at the prospects of uncovering a spy ring and becoming heroes in the process.

Today the fears concerning spies and saboteurs seem silly and perhaps even bordering on paranoid behavior. But it is impossible to judge the long-ago wartime mood of the American people using modern compasses. In the early 1940s Americans were fighting for their lives against a cunning and ruthless enemy. It is no wonder they saw foes everywhere. All strangers were suspected - particularly that man who just moved into the house down the block and who spoke with a foreign accent. War breeds fear and fear gives rise to irrational thoughts and actions.

On the home front, even the nation's children were swept up in the great push for final victory. Boy Scouts and church groups combed city alleys looking for war-winning junk during scrap drives. In farm communities youngsters worked the fields to fill in for family members who were away in the military. It is no wonder that kids too became part of the national alert against spies, saboteurs, and secret agents. Often the young people, driven by powerful imaginations, dreamed of the ultimate act they could perform to secure victory: Yes, they would catch a spy or saboteur before he could commit his evil deed. Thus the kids would join the adult world and do their part to win the war.